TALES OF THE TROJAN WAR

Retold by Kamini Khanduri

Illustrated by Jeff Anderson

Designed by Kathy Ward

Series Editor: Felicity Brooks

SCHOLASTIC INC.

New York Toronto London Auckland Sydney
Mexico City New Delhi Hong Kong Buenos Aires

CONTENTS

Chapter one

THE BEAUTY CONTEST

"Welcome, everybody. Welcome to you all," said Nereus, the sea god, graciously. He was busy greeting the last few guests to the wedding of his daughter, Thetis.

The celebrations in the vast banqueting hall were already in full flow, and everyone was having a wonderful time. Thetis was marrying King Peleus, so it was quite an occasion. Hundreds of well-known people had been invited, and so had all the important gods and goddesses. All, that is, except one.

The happy couple had decided that Eris, the unpopular goddess of spite, might cause trouble and spoil their wedding day, so they had purposely left her off the guest list. But the lack of an invitation didn't stop Eris. She turned up anyway, in a terrible rage, and stormed her way through the mingling guests.

"How dare you!" she screamed in fury, wagging a bony finger at the bride and bridegroom. "How dare you insult me like this! I suppose you thought you'd get away with it, didn't you? Well, you underestimated me, you fools! I'll make you pay for this – just you wait and see!"

As she spoke, she reached

inside her long, black cloak and pulled out a gleaming golden apple. She hesitated briefly, looking around with a hideous scowl on her face. Then, with a shrill cackle, she flung the apple onto the marble floor and flounced out of the hall.

For a moment, everyone stood there in shocked silence. Then Nereus bent down and picked up the apple. He turned it over in his hand.

"There's writing on it!" he exclaimed. " '*For the fairest*'," he read aloud. "That's what it says. '*For the fairest*'."

He looked up. "So, who is it for then? Who's going to claim this golden apple?"

Again, there was silence. Then the deep voice of Hera, queen of the gods, rang out through the hall.

"Well, it's for me, of course! There's no doubt about it. I'm the most beautiful, so the golden apple is mine."

"Yours!" said Athene, the goddess of wisdom and war. "Why should it be yours? Anyone with eyes in their head can see that the apple is meant for me."

Aphrodite, the goddess of love, was not going to stand for this. "Ladies, ladies," she purred sweetly. "What can you be thinking of? *Everyone* knows that when it comes to beauty, no one can compete with me. The apple is mine and that's all there is to it." And she laughed a tinkly little laugh and fluttered her unusually long eyelashes.

Feeling rather confused, all the guests turned to face Zeus. He was the king of the gods and also Hera's husband. Whenever there was a decision to be made, he could generally be relied upon to make it.

This time, though, Zeus was in a tricky position. If he agreed that Hera was the fairest, people would accuse him of putting his own wife first. But if he chose another goddess, Hera would be wild with jealousy. So, after a few moments' thought, he came up with a crafty plan.

"Why is it always me who has to make the decisions?" he grumbled. "Why not let someone else have a try? What about. . . hmm. . . let me see. . . what's the name of that handsome shepherd who lives on Mount Ida? Paris, isn't it? Yes, Paris — a fine young man with impeccable taste, I'm sure. I hereby decree that Paris shall be the judge of this contest. Now, enough of this squabbling. On with the party!"

And, apart from Hera, Athene and Aphrodite exchanging the occasional hostile glance, the wedding celebrations continued without further ado.

apple, but before the shepherd boy could open his mouth, Hera spoke.

"Young man," she proclaimed, in her most queenly tones, "if you choose me, as I'm *sure* you will, I will give you all the power and wealth you could ever ask for."

Not to be outdone, Athene chimed in, "And if you choose me, as I *know* you will, I will give you success in war."

One day, not long after the wedding, Paris was sitting on a grassy knoll on Mount Ida watching his sheep, when Hermes, the messenger of the gods, suddenly appeared. And with him were Hera, Athene and Aphrodite. All three were dressed in their finest robes and looked radiantly lovely, standing there in the dazzling sunlight. Paris was speechless with fear and amazement.

"Paris," announced Hermes, "don't be afraid. Zeus has decided that you are to be the judge of a very important contest. You must give this apple to whichever you think is the most beautiful of these goddesses."

He handed Paris the golden

Aphrodite just smiled sweetly at Paris and whispered softly in his ear, "*When* you choose me, I will give you the most beautiful woman in the world as your wife."

"Now make your choice," ordered Hermes.

Paris stood stock-still, hardly daring to breathe. He glanced nervously at the three powerful goddesses in front of him. Then, after what seemed like a lifetime, he passed the apple to Aphrodite.

Hera and Athene were beside themselves with rage and disappointment. Hera pointed resentfully at Paris. "A beautiful wife won't get you anywhere, you idiotic boy. Just you wait and see!"

"You'll regret this," Athene added in a warning tone. "One day you'll wish you had me to help you. But it's your choice, I suppose!"

Then, just as suddenly as they had appeared, they vanished, along with Hermes.

Aphrodite held the apple up to the sun and sighed happily. Then she stepped forward and spoke to the bewildered young shepherd.

"The most beautiful woman in the world is Helen," she told him. "She lives in Greece, at the court of Menelaus, the king of Sparta. In due course, you will go there and she will fall in love with you, just as I have promised. But now I must leave you."

The goddess disappeared and Paris settled down to watch his sheep again, full of hope that, one day, he might marry the most beautiful woman in the world.

Several years passed, and Paris began to doubt that anything would ever come of the goddess's promise. He was becoming a little bored with his shepherd's lifestyle and yearned for some excitement. So he decided to go down the mountain and visit the nearby city of Troy. He'd heard that King Priam was holding a games

contest there, and Paris thought he'd enter some of the competitions.

When he arrived in the city, he followed the crowds until he reached the huge field where the games were about to begin. Paris entered as many events as he could and, to his amazement, he won nearly all of them. Years of scrambling up and down the mountainside had made his legs immensely strong, and he also discovered that he was a very fast runner. He even managed to beat the king's burly son, Hector. The king and queen were most impressed.

"What a fine young man," said King Priam. "I wonder who he is?"

"He looks strangely familiar," said his daughter, Princess Cassandra. "I have a peculiar feeling that I've seen him before somewhere."

King Priam and Queen Hecuba looked at each other. Cassandra had special powers and could see things that other people couldn't.

"Well, let's call him over and find out," suggested Priam.

As Paris approached the royal party, Cassandra kept her eyes fixed on his face. When he was only a few steps away, she let out a shriek, ran forward and flung her arms around his neck.

"Cassandra!" cried Hecuba, looking shocked. "What *are* you doing?"

"Mother, don't you recognize

him? Can't you see who it is?"

"No," said Hecuba. "I've never seen him before in my life. You really are behaving very oddly, dear."

"But it's *Paris!*" said Cassandra in exasperation.

Paris was very surprised at this. How on earth did this strange woman know his name?

Meanwhile, Priam and Hecuba were staring at the swarthy youth in front of them. Many years ago, they had had a baby son who they'd named Paris. When he was born, the gods had predicted that he would bring destruction to his own city. The king and queen loved their baby, but knew they could not risk such disaster, so they reluctantly gave orders for Paris to be taken to the nearby mountainside and left to die. Surely this boy couldn't be. . .

"Tell me, young man," said King Priam, "where are you from?"

"Mount Ida, sir," replied Paris.

"And what do you do there?"

"I'm a shepherd."

"Who are your parents?"

"My parents are dead, sir, but they were shepherds, too."

"And your name. . ?"

Paris began to feel uneasy. He had always known that the shepherds who brought him up were not his *real* parents. They'd explained to him that they'd found him on the hillside as a baby, and assumed he must be a gift from the gods. When the goddess Demeter visited his mother in a dream to tell her the child's name, they were even more convinced.

"Well. . ." said Paris finally, "my name's Paris."

Hecuba gasped. "He must have been rescued by the shepherds," she whispered. "Oh, Priam – he's alive after all these years!"

The king and queen were so thrilled to be reunited with their long lost son that they put the gods' prediction out of their minds, and Paris was welcomed with open arms.

The young prince spent the following few months getting to know his family. Priam was very anxious that his son shouldn't feel like an outsider, so one day, he summoned Paris to his chamber.

"My dear son," he said. "I want you to know how happy you've made us by coming back after all these years. To show you how much we love and trust you, I'm sending you on a very important mission. Many years ago, my sister, Hesione, was captured by the Greeks. Now I want you to sail to Greece in my best ship and bring her back to Troy."

Paris's heart filled up with excitement and pride. "Really?" he asked, amazed. "Are you really sure

Greece, with a group of Priam's best soldiers as companions.

So much time had gone by that Paris had almost forgotten about Aphrodite's promise that he would marry the most beautiful woman in the world. But the goddess hadn't forgotten.

you want *me* to go — not Hector?"

"Of course!" replied Priam, with an indulgent smile. "It's your chance to prove yourself."

Paris kneeled down in front of the king. "Thank you, Father!" he beamed. "I'll do the best I can – I won't let you down, I promise. Just tell me when you want me to leave."

When Cassandra heard this plan, she begged her father not to let Paris go. She said she could see that the trip would bring terrible trouble to Troy. But now that Paris had been promised the mission, Priam and Hecuba didn't feel they could let him down, so they ignored her. Several days later, after a great deal of preparation, Paris set sail for

Aphrodite watched over Paris carefully, and when she saw his ship approaching the Greek shore, she blew gently into the sail so that it veered off course and had to make an unexpected stop near Sparta, the city of King Menelaus.

When the king heard that a Trojan prince was in the area, he sent a message inviting him and his friends to visit the palace. The Trojans accepted, and on their arrival, they were met by Menelaus and his wife – Helen.

She truly *was* the most beautiful woman Paris had ever seen. Her face was perfect in every way, with a full, curvy mouth and sparkling brown eyes, and her thick, shiny hair flowed around her head in ringlets and curls. But beauty had not brought her happiness. She did love Menelaus, but he was older than her, and sometimes she found him a little boring. She longed for excitement and adventure.

As soon as Helen set eyes upon the handsome Paris, she decided he was much more exciting than her husband. And when Paris saw how unbelievably beautiful she was, he forgot all about rescuing Hesione. All he could think of was Helen.

For the following ten days, Menelaus entertained the Trojans most generously. No host could have been kinder or more attentive to his guests' needs. They feasted on delicious food and drank cup after cup of fine wine. And all the time, Helen and Paris were exchanging furtive glances, longing to speak to each other in private.

On the tenth day, Menelaus summoned his guests.

"My friends," he said. "I have some unfortunate news. An urgent message has arrived from Crete and I must go there at once. However, there's no reason for you to leave. My dear wife is here to take care of you and see that you have all you need. I leave you in her capable hands."

That afternoon, Menelaus set off for Crete. No sooner had the palace gates closed behind him than Paris sneaked away from his companions and tiptoed along the corridors to Helen's room. He found her sitting alone, combing her lovely hair. For a moment he lingered in the doorway, watching in silence. Then he coughed quietly. Helen jumped.

"Sir!" she gasped, flushing red with embarrassment. "You mustn't come to my room! It's not right. Please go back to your friends and your feasting."

Paris ignored her. He took a few steps into the room.

"Helen. . ." he said, desperately. "Helen, you must realize I love you. How can I possibly enjoy myself while you belong to another man?"

Helen opened her mouth to speak, but Paris went on. "I'm eaten up with jealousy every time I even *think* about Menelaus," he said, rushing across the room and taking Helen's hands. "Let me take you away from here, across the sea to Troy."

"Oh Paris," wailed Helen, her eyes filling up with tears. "Don't ask me to do such a thing!" She snatched her hands away guiltily. "It would be terribly wrong to leave my husband and my home," she said. "What would people say? I'd never be able to hold my head up again. But. . . " she let out a strangled sob,

"I can't bear the thought of you leaving. I want to be with you, Paris. Oh, what shall I do?" Tears began to roll down her cheeks.

"We'll go to my father," said Paris decisively. "I'll explain the situation to him and he'll help us. Trust me – it will be all right."

Helen felt as if she were being torn in two. She couldn't bear to think of poor Menelaus's reaction when he found out she'd gone. She knew how much he loved her, and she didn't want to hurt him.

But how often did she get the chance to be swept off her feet by such a gorgeous man? How could she resist Paris's good looks, and the offer of an escape from Sparta? The choice seemed impossible to make.

But Paris wouldn't give up. He stayed in her room until late into the evening, begging her to go with him.

In the end, she agreed.

That night, while everyone else was asleep, Helen, Paris and his companions crept away from the palace and boarded the Trojan ship. They raised the sail as quickly as they could, then, softly and silently, they sailed away over the dark blue sea.

When Menelaus returned a few days later, he strode around the palace in search of his wife and guests.

"Helen!" he called. "Helen, where are you?"

The palace servants looked at each other nervously as they went about their work.

"Has anybody seen my wife?" Menelaus asked. No one answered.

"Well, speak up. Where is she?"

Still not one of the servants dared to say anything.

"Will somebody please tell me what is going on?" the king shouted.

At last, an old servant woman mumbled, "She's gone, sir."

"Gone? "Gone where?"

"She went just after you left for Crete, sir. In the night. With the Trojan prince."

"With the Trojan prince? What are you talking about, woman?"

For a moment, Menelaus was confused. Then his confusion turned to anger as the awful truth dawned.

"Is this the same Trojan prince I welcomed into my home?" he snarled from between clenched teeth. "The Trojan prince I entertained with fine food and drink? The charming, handsome, well-dressed Trojan prince?" His voice rose to a bellow.

"TRAITOR!" he roared, storming through the empty hall. "So this is how he repays me! By sneaking away in the night, and taking my wife with him! Cowardly thief! He'll be sorry for this! I'll make him wish he'd never set foot in my palace!"

Helen, Paris and his companions crept away from the palace

Then the king stopped and stood still, trembling. A faithful palace servant came and reached out kindly as if to touch his arm, but Menelaus turned away violently. There were tears in his eyes.

"Helen," he whispered desperately to himself.

"How could you go? How could you leave me?"

His shoulders shook, just a little. Then he pulled himself upright, gritted his teeth and clenched his fists. He turned suddenly back to face the servant, wiped his eyes, and set his features in a furious, determined scowl.

"THIS MEANS *WAR!*" he yelled suddenly. He spotted a young messenger trembling in a nearby doorway.

"You!" he ordered. "Take an urgent message to my brother, King Agamemnon. Tell him to gather together all the Greek leaders. We'll raise an army – a huge, unbeatable army – the biggest army ever! And we'll sail to Troy and wage war on those Trojans until they give me back my wife. No one treats Menelaus like this and gets away with it!"

And with that, he stormed out of the palace.

Meanwhile, Paris and Helen were sailing away over the Aegean Sea. Spiteful Eris looked down on them from her hideaway on Mount Olympus, laughing wickedly.

"My plan worked!" she cried. "This will be the longest and bloodiest war that's ever been fought. Every single god, goddess or mortal – they'll *all* be sorry – very sorry – they insulted me."

And, wrapping her cloak tightly around her, the goddess scurried away to her cave.

Chapter two

PREPARING FOR WAR

King Agamemnon of Mycenae stood gazing around the army camp at Aulis. As soon as he had heard the news from his brother, King Menelaus of Sparta, about what had happened to Helen, he'd promised to do everything he could to help get her back.

Agamemnon was a very experienced leader, and he had been chosen as commander in chief of the Greek fighting force. Hundreds of messages had been sent all over Greece, and most of the leaders had arrived at Aulis with their armies. Thousands of the fittest, strongest men in the country were camped by the shore, ready to set off for Troy.

But Agamemnon knew the war couldn't be won by numbers alone. He needed the strategic skills of King Ulysses of Ithaca. And he knew the prophesy of Chiron the centaur. Chiron had foretold that the Greeks could never beat the Trojans without Achilles, the half-god, half-human son of Thetis and Peleus.

At this very moment, in fact, Agamemnon was waiting for news from his men. They'd been sent to get the two missing heroes, and they certainly seemed to be taking their time over it.

King Ulysses and his wife Queen Penelope were having supper. They'd finished their main course of roast boar, and were starting on some fruit, when there was a loud banging on the palace gates.

"Whoever can that be?" exclaimed Penelope. "I hope they haven't woken the baby."

"Who knows," shrugged Ulysses, biting into a slice of melon.

A few seconds later, a servant appeared in the doorway.

"Sir," he said, "there's a soldier here with an urgent message for you. He's come all the way from Mycenae."

"Very well," said Ulysses. "Show him in."

The soldier marched into the hall, took a deep breath and recited the following message:

"King Ulysses. Come to Aulis at once and bring your army. The Trojans have stolen Menelaus's wife. We are sailing to Troy to wage war on them. Remember your oath to help us. From King Agamemnon of Mycenae."

Ulysses sat up suddenly, looking shocked. He glanced at Penelope.

"Oh, Ulysses," his wife whispered. "You *can't* go – you might be away for years."

"But the oath. . . " he said.

Before Helen had married Menelaus, many of the other Greek leaders, including Ulysses, had wanted to marry her because she was so beautiful. Helen's father had chosen Menelaus as her husband, but he was so worried that her other admirers wouldn't stop chasing his daughter, he had made them all take an oath. They had to vow to leave Helen alone, and to help Menelaus to get her back if anyone should ever kidnap her. A few years after taking the oath, Ulysses had fallen in love with Penelope. Since then, he hadn't given Helen

another thought – until now.

"I can't break my oath," he whispered to his wife. "But it does seem ridiculous to go to war over this. It'll blow over soon anyway. I mean," he added, reassuring himself, "they can't really need me, can they?"

He turned to the messenger. "Tell King Agamemnon I'll. . . send him my reply very soon," he said.

And as soon as the messenger had left, he set to work on a plan.

Several months later, there was another loud knock on the gate. When Penelope was summoned, she found another group of soldiers standing there.

"Queen Penelope?" said their leader.

"Yes," Penelope answered.

"My name's Palamedes, Madam. I've been sent by Menelaus. We're here for your husband."

"Ah," said Penelope. "Just a minute – I'll go and get him."

She slipped back into the palace, leaving the soldiers waiting outside. After some time, they became impatient and were just about to knock again when the queen reappeared with the baby in her arms.

"I'm so sorry," she said, smiling awkwardly. "My husband's in rather a strange mood. . . he seems to have decided to go and work in the fields. Follow me."

She led them around the palace to the fields at the back. In the distance, they saw Ulysses steering a pair of oxen. He was walking along behind them, sowing seeds in the furrows they made. The soldiers watched curiously as he came closer. Then Palamedes turned to Penelope. "Is your husband all right, Madam?" he asked.

Penelope raised her eyebrows.

"I mean," continued Palamedes, "what's he doing sowing the fields? Surely that's servants' work?"

"Wait a minute," said another soldier, peering at the king. "He's not even sowing grain! It looks like some kind of white powder instead."

Penelope sighed.

"Yes," she said wearily. "I think it's salt. I'm afraid he's not been himself over the last few months. His mind is. . . well. . . not what it used to be." Her eyes filled with tears and she lowered her voice to a whisper. "The physicians say he's insane. You won't take him away to war, will you? I really don't think he's up to it and he certainly couldn't be relied upon to make any sensible decisions."

Palamedes scratched his head. He hadn't heard anything about Ulysses losing his mind. Surely the news would have spread if it were true? He gazed out over the field. As he did so, Ulysses glanced up and their eyes met. Something about the other man's expression made Palamedes suspicious.

"Madam," he said to Penelope. "Could I hold your baby for a minute?"

Penelope looked surprised, but passed him the child.

Palamedes began to walk across the field. When he was standing in Ulysses's path, a little way in front of him, he bent down and gently laid the baby on the ground. Then he stepped aside.

Ulysses drove the oxen closer and closer to the spot where the child was lying. The two huge creatures lurched nearer, their hooves crunching the hard earth. The baby merely kicked his legs and gurgled happily.

When the oxen were inches from the baby's head, Penelope let out a piercing scream. Palamedes clenched his fists and looked away.

Then, at the very last second, just before the heavy beasts trampled right over the tiny child, Ulysses let out a dreadful roar, and hit the animals with his stick, forcing them to swerve to one side.

There was a moment of silence. Then the baby began to wail loudly.

As Ulysses ran to pick him up and comfort him, Palamedes trudged slowly back to the edge of the field.

"Your husband's a very clever madman," he said to Penelope.

The soldiers smiled and Penelope looked at the ground.

Ulysses was left with no choice. A few days later, he said a tearful goodbye to his wife and baby, and left for Aulis with an army of men.

Meanwhile, Thetis was soaring through the air on her way to the island of Skyros. Her son, Achilles, clung to her tightly.

"Where are we going?" he shouted, as the wind whipped his face. "Can't we slow down a bit?"

"No," snapped Thetis. Then, when she saw his anxious expression, she added, "I'm sorry, but there's no time to lose. The Greeks have been planning this war for some time now, and they're bound to come looking for you soon."

"Do they want me because I'm such a good soldier?" asked Achilles. Although he was still young, Achilles had quite a high opinion of himself, especially when it came to using weapons. His teacher, Chiron, the wise old centaur, had trained him to be a deadly fighter.

"Probably," smiled Thetis.

"Where are we going?" he shouted

She couldn't tell Achilles the real reason she had to hide him away – Chiron's prediction. The centaur had not only said that the Greek army would need Achilles if they were going to capture the city of Troy. He'd also foretold that Achilles would die fighting there.

At first, Thetis wasn't too worried. After all, Achilles was no ordinary boy. When he was a baby, she'd taken him on a journey to the magical River Styx. She'd crouched down on the muddy river bank and, holding the baby carefully by his tiny heel, had dipped his body into the swirling water.

"There!" she'd whispered, pulling him out and wrapping him in a warm blanket. "Now you'll live forever – just like me."

Thetis had never told her husband, Peleus, what she'd done. As a mortal, he didn't understand the importance of these things. But Thetis was a goddess, and it made her feel much happier knowing that she'd made her precious son immortal too.

Now, though, with all this talk of a major war against Troy, she couldn't afford to take any chances – even though she was sure Achilles couldn't be killed.

"Are we nearly at Skyros yet?" asked Achilles impatiently.

"Yes, dear," said Thetis, kissing his cheek as if he were a baby. "We're nearly there. And I'm going to make sure no one will find you."

One hot afternoon at Aulis, Ulysses burst into Agamemnon's tent.

"Sir!" he said. "Sorry to disturb you, but there's something I think you should know."

Agamemnon looked up. Here was someone he was always pleased to see. From the moment he'd reached Aulis, Ulysses had thrown himself into the preparations with great enthusiasm. Agamemnon had come to rely on his intelligence and bright ideas. If only they could find Achilles, Agamemnon thought, they could get going and set off for Troy.

"What is it, Ulysses?" he asked.

"There's a story going around that Achilles has been seen at the court of King Lycomedes on Skyros. I wondered if you wanted me to go there to try to track him down?"

Agamemnon's eyes lit up. "You must go at once," he said.

A few days later, Ulysses arrived at Skyros laden with wonderful gifts for King Lycomedes and his daughters. After laying these out on a long wooden table, he started questioning his host.

"Is there by any chance a young

man named Achilles at your court?" he asked.

"No," replied Lycomedes, pouring his guest a cup of wine. "I've never met him. But his sister's here. She's one of the young ladies over there with my daughters."

He pointed to the group of girls who were clustered around the table, shrieking with delight as they examined the glittering jewels and fine embroidered material displayed there.

"Which one is she?" asked Ulysses.

"That one at the back – the tall one," said Lycomedes, wondering why his guest was so curious about this particular young lady.

Ulysses looked across the room and saw the girl immediately. She was a head taller than the others and didn't appear very interested in the gifts. In fact, she even looked a little bored and was gazing wistfully out of the window as if she wished she were outside.

When she glanced back at her companions, something seemed to catch her eye. She moved nearer to the table, and, watched closely by Ulysses, stretched out her hand. From under the folds of a sumptuous

21

red cloak that was draped over the gifts, she slowly pulled out a sword with a gleaming bronze blade and a hilt studded with jewels.

Ulysses waited.

The girl lifted the weapon away from the table, raised it above her head and, for a moment, held it motionless. Then she brought it slicing down through the air in one graceful movement.

"Achilles!" called out Ulysses.

The 'girl' spun around, the sword still in her hand. The expression of boredom had disappeared and her eyes shone with excitement. Ulysses knew his suspicion had been right – Achilles's 'sister' was, in fact, Achilles himself in disguise. Thetis had put a spell on him so that no one would recognize him. But the spell had been broken the moment Achilles had heard his own name, and soon everyone began to wonder how they had ever mistaken this tall, handsome young man for a girl.

In the midst of the confusion, Ulysses managed to guide Achilles into a quiet corner of the room. He explained to the boy that he was needed to fight in the war against Troy. Achilles was more than willing. He hated pretending to be a girl, and he was longing to see some action. The idea of a war sounded thrilling.

Without a moment's hesitation, he agreed to go with Ulysses.

At last, Agamemnon was ready to leave Aulis for Troy. A thousand large ships loaded with supplies were lined up along the shore, and an army of a hundred thousand men was gathered at the camp. They'd come from all corners of Greece, some tramping for months across rough, uneven ground, over steep hills and mountains, and through thick cypress forests.

Most of the soldiers had started out full of energy and keen to fight. But as the weeks had turned into months and the months into years, they'd lost their enthusiasm and grown bored and frustrated. Rumbles of discontent were spreading around the camp, and Agamemnon knew that if the war didn't start soon, there'd be trouble.

But there was still one problem – there was no wind. And without wind, the ships couldn't sail. Dreading the idea of more delays, Agamemnon had summoned old Calchas, the soothsayer, in the hope that he'd be able to explain.

"Where in Zeus's name is he!" muttered Agamemnon, drumming his fingers impatiently on the table. "He's always late."

Menelaus stood up and went to look outside.

"He's on his way," he said, as he came back in. "He's shuffling across the field, mumbling some nonsense to himself."

The other leaders smiled. A few minutes later, there was a rustling in the doorway.

"Ah, Calchas," Agamemnon said. "Here you are at last. Come in, come in. Now, you probably know why we've called you here. It's this wind – it just won't start blowing. Any idea what the problem is?"

"Er. . . yes. . . but, to be honest, sir, it's not very good news," said Calchas, staring uneasily at the ground.

"Not good news? What are you talking about?" the king demanded.

"Well, the thing is. . . it's Artemis," continued Calchas.

"Artemis? What about her?"

"She's. . . she's angry with you," said Calchas with a sinking feeling in the pit of his stomach.

"Angry? With me? What on earth for?"

"Apparently you've killed one of her sacred deer."

Agamemnon looked around at the others with an expression of surprise on his face and then laughed loudly. "More likely she's jealous because I'm a better hunter than her!" he snorted.

"Sir!" gasped Calchas in horror. "If she hears you saying that, there's no telling what she'll do. You *know* what a temper she has."

"All right, all right, I'll try to make amends. What does she want? An old goat sacrificed to her and a lot of weeping and wailing and praying?" Agamemnon smiled to himself – gods and goddesses were so predictable. "I'm right, aren't I?"

"Well, not exactly, sir," mumbled Calchas.

"Not exactly? Not exactly? Then *what* exactly, you old fool. Come on – I haven't got all day to sit here listening to you rambling on. Get to the point."

"Agamemnon. . ." Menelaus began. "Let's not argue about it. Do whatever Artemis wants, so we can leave for Troy and get Helen back."

"Absolutely," said Agamemnon. "Come on Calchas, I do have a war to fight, you know. Just tell me how I can please Artemis, so she'll make the wind blow. Then we can all get on with what we've come here for."

Calchas breathed deeply, trying to stay calm.

"She *does* want you to make a sacrifice," he began.

"There! I knew it!" crowed the king.

"But she won't be satisfied with a goat," continued Calchas.

"All right, two goats, ten goats, a cow, a flock of sheep – what, in the name of the gods, *does* she want?"

"Your daughter," blurted Calchas.

Agamemnon stared at him, open-mouthed.

"What?"

"She wants your daughter, Iphigenia," Calchas repeated.

"Iphigenia?" Agamemnon said very quietly. He was almost whispering. "Iphigenia?"

He looked confused, frightened and suddenly much older. He gazed around the tent, as if hoping the other leaders might be able to help.

"I. . . there must be some mistake?" he pleaded, turning to Calchas.

The soothsayer raised his head and looked Agamemnon in the eye.

"No, sir," he said sadly. "There's no mistake. Artemis will only forgive you if you sacrifice your daughter."

"But – how can I? I mean –

she's just a sweet young girl. She's never harmed anyone in her life. The poor girl won't understand. What will I say to her? How will I explain?" And then a look of absolute horror flickered across his face. "What will I say to her *mother?*"

Nobody said anything. There was nothing they could say.

After staring vacantly into space for a few

seconds, Agamemnon stood up. With a last, desperate glance at Calchas, he gathered his cloak around his shoulders, picked up his helmet and walked slowly and unsteadily out of the tent.

⚔⚔⚔⚔⚔⚔⚔⚔⚔⚔⚔⚔

The news spread like wildfire, from soldier to soldier and from tent to tent. Soon, the whole camp was buzzing with snatches of whispered conversations:

"Have you heard? Agamemnon's going to sacrifice his daughter. . ."

"They say he's trying to get out of it, but the others are insisting it's the only way we'll get to Troy. . ." ·

"Well, I'm not going home without a war. . ."

"But his own *daughter*. . ."

"He's sent for the girl – told her mother he's found her a husband!"

"Imagine! Coming all this way thinking you're going to meet your husband. . ."

"The way I see it, there's a thousand ships ready to go, and a lot of angry men ready to fight. If Agamemnon calls off the war, they might just turn against him. . ."

"The girl's arrived. She's very pretty. . ."

"The mother's found out. She's raging around like a madwoman. . ."

"The daughter's weeping and begging her father. He must be a hard-hearted man."

"What would you do? Cancel the war and risk a full-scale battle starting here?"

"I've just heard – it's official. The sacrifice is to take place tomorrow, on the shore. You'll have to get there early if you want a good view. . ."

"My daughter's about the same age as that poor girl. . ."

"We'll soon be off to Troy!"

⚔⚔⚔⚔⚔⚔⚔⚔⚔⚔⚔⚔

Iphigenia stood beside the makeshift altar, her face half-hidden behind her long, dark hair. She was no longer crying – she had used up all her tears pleading with her father. He had explained that, although it broke his heart, he had to obey the goddess. Try as she might, Iphigenia couldn't understand at all. She'd always been so sure that her father loved her more than anything in the world. Surely he wouldn't really be able to do such a terrible thing?

Meanwhile her mother, Clytemnestra, was standing beside her, seething with rage. She would not look at her husband, but her eyes burned with hatred. She made a silent vow that one day she'd make him pay for putting his country before his own child.

Agamemnon showed no emotion. But those who looked

closely saw that as he picked up the knife, his hand was shaking.

With almost the whole Greek army watching from a respectful distance, he slowly approached his daughter.

"Silence!" called a herald.

The crowd hardly breathed. The only sound was the waves lapping against the shore as Iphigenia closed her eyes and bent her head forward. Agamemnon raised the knife, while Clytemnestra, powerless to intervene, shook with grief and fury.

There was a moment of stillness. Agamemnon swallowed hard and tightened his grip on the handle. The blade glistened in the morning sun as it started to move. . .

Suddenly there was a huge flash of light. The knife clattered to the ground, and Agamemnon stepped back in fright. Iphigenia screamed, then vanished into thin air. And there, in front of the altar, instead of the girl, was a baby deer!

As the crowd gasped in amazement, Clytemnestra looked wildly around until her eye fell upon Calchas.

"What's happening?" she screamed. "Where's my daughter?"

Calchas sighed and slowly made his way to the altar. After inspecting the deer closely, he said, "I think it's all right, madam. Yes – everything seems to be all right."

"All right? What do you mean, all right? She's *disappeared*. How on earth can that be *all right?*" sobbed Clytemnestra.

"She'll be safe now. No one will harm her. Artemis must have taken pity on her at the last minute and decided to make do with a deer instead. I've seen this happen before," nodded Calchas wisely.

"But where is she?" hissed Clytemnestra, infuriated at the old man's lack of urgency.

"She's probably been taken to one of Artemis's temples, to be a priestess there. That's what usually happens in cases like this."

"And when will I see her again?"

There was a pause.

"You probably won't, madam. But you can be sure that she'll be well looked after."

Clytemnestra was speechless. First she'd had to face up to her daughter being sacrificed, then she saw her vanish before her very eyes, and now this irritating old man was saying she'd never see her again. It was all too much. After taking a last, long look at the altar, as if she hoped Iphigenia might suddenly reappear, Clytemnestra began to walk slowly back to the tents.

When she was some distance away, Agamemnon turned to Calchas.

"So what do we do now?" he asked, sounding very weary. "I've lost my daughter and there's still no wind blowing."

"We sacrifice the deer instead," replied the old man.

So they quickly performed the sacrifice to Artemis, following Calchas's instructions, and the deer's blood began to drip onto the altar.

Agamemnon held his breath.

At first nothing happened. Then suddenly, he became aware of a very gentle breeze on his face.

"It's not strong enough," he said to Calchas. "I can hardly feel it."

"Be patient, sir," replied the soothsayer, placing the deer's body on the fire.

The flames crackled loudly and smoke began to rise. As Agamemnon stared into the fire, he felt the breeze ruffle his hair a little.

"Come on, come on!" he muttered.

Then, very, very slowly, the smoke started billowing out across the sand, and the dry grass that grew behind the beach started to sway from side to side.

"At last!" whispered Agamemnon. "At last!" And, heaving a huge sigh of relief, he began to hurry back in the direction of the camp.

The wind grew stronger and stronger throughout the day, and the next morning, it was still blowing hard. The goddess Artemis had kept to her promise. The conditions were perfect for a sea voyage.

So, several years after the Trojan prince, Paris, had stolen away with Helen in the middle of the night, an army of one hundred thousand Greek men climbed on board, and the sails were unfurled.

Not knowing what horrors or glories might await them there, uncertain whether they would ever win back the beautiful Helen, but full of excitement and lust for war, the soldiers and their leaders gazed ahead at the horizon as a thousand Greek ships set sail for Troy.

Chapter three

THE ARGUMENT

Achilles stood in the doorway of his tent, gazing out at the world. The sun was high in the sky, and all around was the hustle and bustle of the camp. To the left, the sandy beach curved in a golden arc along the water's edge. Rows of black ships stood on the shore, their huge hulls partly buried in the sand, their masts creaking in the summer breeze. And away to the east, across a wide grassy plain, stood the high walls and towers of Troy itself, gleaming in the distance.

Achilles sighed and cast his mind back. He remembered the long, rough sea crossing from Greece; his first glimpse of this land, and the daunting sight of the fortified city.

What excitement he'd felt as they all disembarked and unloaded the horses, tents, weapons and supplies; how certain he'd been that they would fight their way into the city and capture it; and how proudly he had led his soldiers into battle for the very first time.

He turned and looked across the plain. Somewhere, among those golden towers, was Helen herself. Perhaps she was wandering through a sunlit room, or resting in a walled garden, away from the noise of the battlefield. Achilles felt frustrated. Menelaus's beautiful wife, the cause of all this conflict, was so near, and yet impossible to reach.

"We must find a way in," he

muttered to himself, as he stepped back into the tent. "We *must.*"

"What's that?" asked his closest friend, Patroclus, who was sitting on a stool mending his bow.

"I just can't believe we've been here all this time and still haven't found a way into Troy," said Achilles.

"Well, no one could accuse us of not trying," said Patroclus.

"I know," sighed Achilles. Patroclus was right. Every time the Trojan army marched out of the gates to defend their city, the Greeks were there on the plain, fighting as hard as they could.

"But they always seem to force us back," continued Patroclus. "I don't know how they do it – their army's half the size of ours. Still, if anyone can beat them, it's you."

Achilles smiled.

"You're by far the best soldier," said Patroclus. "Everyone says so."

For a moment, Achilles let his mind wander again. The noise of battle filled his head: swords clashing against shields, arrows whistling through the air, voices shouting orders. His muscles grew tense and a thrill of excitement ran through his body. If only I could find Paris on the battlefield, thought Achilles. I'd like to see how long that cowardly, wife-stealing little traitor would last against my sword!

Patroclus interrupted his daydream.

"Just can't seem to starve them out either," he said, holding his bow up to the light to examine the repair.

For ages now, the Greeks had been raiding the villages in the area and stealing all the food. No one could understand what the Trojans were living off.

"Well, they must be getting food from somewhere," Achilles said, kicking frustratedly at the ground.

"Maybe," suggested Patroclus, "we're doing something wrong - maybe Agamemnon's not keeping the gods happy."

Suddenly a shout went up from outside the tent.

"The gates are opening! The Trojans are coming out!"

"Good!" said Achilles. "Pass me my helmet. *This* time I'm really going to go for it!"

"Maybe tomorrow we'll be marching triumphantly through Troy!" said Patroclus, standing aside to let Achilles through the tent opening.

"Let's hope so," said Achilles, gritting his teeth as he stepped out into the sunlight.

Meanwhile, on the slopes of Mount Olympus, Apollo was sitting under a shady olive tree, lazily strumming his lyre. Beside him on the grass, his silver bow and arrows glinted in the dappled sunlight that made its way through the foliage. Sparrows were chirping merrily in the branches above and a gentle breeze rustled the leaves.

As he fingered the strings of the instrument, Apollo hummed a tune.

"La la da daaaa. . . "

He paused for a minute. Something had distracted him. He listened hard but heard nothing.

"La la da daaaaaa. . . "

He stopped again. This time, he was certain he'd heard something. And sure enough, after a few minutes, the faint sound of a man's voice came wafting through the air.

"Apollo!" it called. "Lord Apollo, can you hear me?"

Apollo groaned. It was Chryses, the priest at one of his temples.

"Oh what does *he* want!" grumbled Apollo, placing his lyre carefully on the grass and struggling to his feet.

"Lord Apollo! It's me, Chryses. Are you there?"

"Yes, I'm here!" shouted Apollo. "What's the matter?"

"It's my daughter," replied Chryses. His voice sounded a little louder now. "The Greek soldiers came rampaging through the country and raided the temple and they've taken her away. They've stolen your statue and lots of treasures but I wouldn't have troubled you about those. And then. . . " his voice started to quiver, "they found Chryseis – my lovely daughter – hiding behind the altar. She was crying and screaming, and I begged them to leave her alone. But they dragged her back to their camp."

"Have you tried speaking to someone in charge?" asked Apollo.

"Yes," replied Chryses. "The very next day, I gathered up all the treasures I had left, and went to see

For a moment, Achilles let his mind wander. . .

The noise of battle filled his head

King Agamemnon. I pleaded with him to give back my daughter and offered him a whole sackful of gifts in return. But. . . but. . . "

"But what?" asked Apollo. "What did he say?"

"He said the soldiers had given Chryseis to him and he liked her so much, he wanted to keep her as his special servant. He even said. . . "

The birds were singing loudly and Apollo had to strain to hear the old man.

"He even said that he was going to take her back to Greece with him." Chryses' voice rose to a wail.

"Does Agamemnon realize who you are?" asked Apollo.

"Yes he does," replied Chryses. "I told him I was one of your priests and that you'd be angry if he didn't give my daughter back."

"I *am* angry," said Apollo. "Leave it with me. I'll deal with it – don't you worry."

"Oh thank you, Apollo," called Chryses, sounding very relieved. "I knew you'd help."

Apollo waited a few minutes but heard nothing more. He sighed loudly and sank down onto the grass again. After a moment's hesitation, he picked up his lyre.

"Just a couple more songs and then I'll start work on a plan," he thought to himself. "A few extra minutes won't make any difference."

He leaned back against the tree and started strumming.

Back at the Greek camp, Agamemnon was getting impatient. He'd called all the leaders to his tent for an urgent meeting with Calchas the soothsayer. But Calchas, as usual, was late.

"Where is he?" he grumbled. "As if we don't all have better things to do than sit around waiting for him."

"He's an old man, sir," said Achilles. "I suppose he can't walk very fast."

Agamemnon snorted. "Well, I'm tired of waiting. We'll make a start without him. Ulysses, what's the latest news on this sickness?"

In the past few days, a deadly disease had been spreading through the camp. Ulysses had been trying to find out what was causing it.

"It's horrible," he shuddered. "I still don't know what it is, but I know I don't want to catch it. They all have the same symptoms – exhaustion, shaking limbs, staring eyes. Then they keel over and die. And the whole process happens within a day. I've never seen anything like it before."

Agamemnon frowned. His brother Menelaus looked worried. "I hope the gods are on our side, Agamemnon," he began. "You haven't done anything to upset them, have you? I mean—"

"Ah, Calchas!" Agamemnon interrupted. "Here at last. Come on in."

Calchas hovered in the doorway, leaning on his stick and looking around nervously. Then, with everyone's eyes on him, he made his way slowly to the middle of the tent.

"Now," said Agamemnon briskly, "I'm sure you know about this strange sickness that's spreading around the camp. Well, I want to know why it's happening and how to put a stop to it."

Calchas took a deep breath and tried to stay calm. But as he cleared his throat to speak, he was overcome by his usual nerves and he couldn't get rid of the tremor in his voice.

"It's, um. . . Apollo, sir," he mumbled.

"What?" shouted the king. "I can't hear you. Speak up."

"I said, it's Apollo," said Calchas, far too loudly.

"Apollo? What about Apollo?"

"He's. . . angry with you," said Calchas.

"Oh," said Agamemnon, looking slightly embarrassed and avoiding his brother's eyes. "What have I done this time? Come on, spit it out!"

"It's to do with your new servant girl, sir – Chryseis."

Calchas paused and glanced warily at Agamemnon. The king said nothing, so the old man continued:

"Her father was very upset that you wouldn't give her back so he told Apollo what had happened. Apollo was so angry, he sent a plague. That's why all the soldiers are dying."

"So what do I have to do to be forgiven?" Agamemnon asked huffily. "Another sacrifice, I suppose?"

"No," said Calchas. "He just wants you to give the girl back to her father."

At this, Agamemnon looked annoyed. "I don't think that'll be necessary," he said decisively. "A sacrifice would be much more suitable, I'm sure."

The truth was, Agamemnon wanted to keep Chryseis. She was an excellent servant, and she was also very beautiful. Agamemnon liked the idea that, as commander, he should have the best-looking servant girl of all.

There was a pause during which the other leaders exchanged glances. Calchas kept his eyes fixed firmly on the ground.

Then Achilles spoke.

"Sir," he said. "You have other servant girls. Is she really so special?"

"Are you arguing with me, Achilles?" growled Agamemnon.

"No," said Achilles. "It's just with so many men dying, it seems only right to give the girl back."

"Oh, it seems only right, does it?" said the king in icy tones. "Well, Achilles. I'll tell you what I'll do. I'll give the girl back – on one condition."

Achilles looked pleased – he hadn't thought Agamemnon would give in so easily.

"What's that, sir?" he asked.

"That you give me *your* girl instead," replied Agamemnon.

"Look," said Menelaus hurriedly, "let's not get into a fight. There's a lot at stake – we should concentrate on the war and getting Helen back."

"He's right," added Ulysses wisely. "We'll never win if we stand here bickering."

Agamemnon ignored them.

"I've seen that girl of yours around," he went on, still talking to Achilles.

"She's very pretty, isn't she? Not quite as pretty as Chryseis, of course, but she'll do. What's her name? Bristia? Brismene?"

"It's Briseis," said Achilles quietly.

"Ah Briseis. Yes. Good. Well, that's all right then."

"Sir," said Achilles. "I'm afraid I can't agree to this."

"What do you mean, you can't agree!" exploded the king. "I don't care whether you agree or not. *I'm* in charge here. *I* make the decisions and *I* say we'll discuss this no further."

He looked around the tent. "You can all go now."

Achilles went white. He took a breath as if to speak again, but the king spoke first.

"I said, you can go!" he roared.

"Sir," said Achilles, shaking with rage. "If you do this, I will withdraw from the fighting and order all my soldiers to do the same."

"Do as you please," said Agamemnon

coldly. "I'll send my heralds over to your tent to pick up the girl."

"All right," Achilles growled. "Have it your own way." He gazed around at the other leaders, his dark eyes flashing with anger. No one dared say a word. Then, with one last furious glare in Agamemnon's direction, he stood up and stormed out of the tent.

Achilles's mother, the goddess Thetis, was perched on top of a rock in the middle of the Aegean Sea, watching the dolphins playing. She loved the way they leaped right out of the water, their smooth, shiny bodies so graceful and streamlined. Sometimes, they swam up to her rock and bobbed around with only their heads above the surface. She reached out and patted the nearest one. As the animal swam away, Thetis decided she would turn herself into a dolphin.

She was just getting to her feet when she suddenly felt very cold. She shivered and folded her arms around her body.

Thetis knew what that strange chilly feeling meant. Something was wrong with Achilles. She could always tell when her son was in trouble. Now that all her efforts to keep him away from the war had

failed, and Achilles was at Troy, this could mean something serious.

Thetis immediately turned herself into a seagull and flew as fast as she could across the sea to the Trojan shore. She looked down at the Greek ships lined up on the beach below, and the rows of tents. She turned and swooped down. Landing softly just outside Achilles's tent, she quickly changed back to her normal shape and crept inside.

Achilles was sitting hunched on the ground, staring sulkily at the floor. He looked up grumpily when he heard the tent flap rustle, and was startled to see his mother.

"Mother? Why are *you* here?" he demanded.

Thetis bustled over and gave Achilles a hug.

"Just looking after my little boy, that's all," she twittered. She was relieved to find he wasn't injured. "What's wrong, my darling?"

"Nothing," mumbled Achilles.

"Now come on, dear," Thetis said. "I'm your mother! I know something's the matter."

"It's that Agamemnon," fumed Achilles suddenly. "How dare he treat me like this? I'm his finest soldier – everyone says so – you'd think he'd respect me. Instead. . ." Achilles was so outraged, he almost felt like bursting into tears.

"What?" asked Thetis. "What did he do to my Achilles?"

So Achilles told his mother all about the argument, and how the king's heralds had come to his tent and taken Briseis away.

"And I've refused to fight any more," he concluded at last. "I've withdrawn all my soldiers and I hope the army's struggling without us. I never thought I'd say that, Mother – I so much wanted us to capture Troy – but he's made me furious. . . treating me like a nobody, shouting at me as if I were a child – how *dare* he?"

"It's outrageous, that's what it is!" agreed Thetis when Achilles had finished his story. "That silly old commander just doesn't appreciate you, my darling, and I've a good mind to tell him so! In fact," she murmured, a sly smile spreading across her face, "I'd like to teach him a proper lesson."

"Look, Mother," said Achilles anxiously. "Don't do anything silly, will you? I mean—"

"Silly? Me?" asked Thetis. "Of course not. I'm just going to pull a few strings, that's all! You leave it to me, dear!" And before Achilles could say another word, she was gone.

It was early in the morning and Zeus was trying to sit very still on his throne while Aphrodite combed all the tangles out of his hair. "Do stop fidgeting, Father!"

she said irritably.

"Well, it's taking so long," grumbled Zeus. "And it hurts!"

"If you'd let me comb it more often, it wouldn't get so tangled. I comb mine every day and see how smooth and silky it is?"

Aphrodite tossed her head so that her dark curls tumbled over her shoulders. Zeus smiled. He was just about to tell her how pretty she was when Hermes marched in.

"There's someone here to see you, Father," he announced loudly.

"Who is it?" asked Zeus. "Ah, Thetis! What a pleasant surprise. What can I do for you?"

Thetis ran across the golden floor and kneeled at Zeus's feet.

"Oh Zeus, it's Achilles," she said. "He's been treated very badly by Agamemnon and I was wondering if you might. . . be able to help?" She squeezed his hand imploringly.

"That depends on what you want me to do," said Zeus, peering anxiously at the doorway. If Hera came in and saw Thetis holding his hand, there would be trouble.

"I want you to punish Agamemnon by letting the Trojans win the war," said Thetis sweetly.

"Ah," said Zeus, scratching his beard. "I'm not sure Hera would be very happy about that – you know she hates the Trojans after all that business with Paris and the apple. . . "

"Well don't tell her then!" suggested Aphrodite, beaming at Thetis. "I think it's a good idea."

"Hmm. . . I don't know," said Zeus. The Trojans *did* steal Helen."

"*Please*," begged Thetis, gazing up at him. "It breaks my heart to see my son so unhappy." And her eyes filled with tears.

"All right, all right," said Zeus kindly. "Leave it with me."

"Oh thank you, Zeus," said Thetis, flashing a grateful smile at Aphrodite.

"Ah, that'll be Hera," said Zeus, hearing familiar footsteps. He shook off Thetis's hand and jumped to his feet. "I think I'll go and meet her."

As he hurried out, Athene, the tall, beautiful goddess of wisdom and war, entered the room. She looked suspiciously at Aphrodite and Thetis, who were smiling coyly.

"What's going on?" she challenged them. "You're not interfering in the war again, I hope?"

"Oh, it's not us," laughed Thetis. "It's not our fault if Zeus decides to help the Trojans along a little, is it, Aphrodite dear?"

"But the Greeks should win!" said Athene angrily. "You know they're the ones who've been wronged!"

"We don't know any such thing, actually," said Aphrodite sweetly. And taking Thetis by the arm, she swept out of the room.

Chapter four

THE DUEL

Far from the city walls, deep inside the city of Troy, Helen was standing at her loom weaving a big, bright wall hanging. She'd been working on it ever since she'd arrived at King Priam's palace all those years ago.

At first, she'd been happy enough. Priam and his son Hector were kind to her, and she was so excited about being with Paris that she didn't really care where she was.

But as time had passed, she'd begun to feel a little homesick. Paris seemed to spend most of his days out with his friends, and Helen had to admit that he wasn't as wonderful as she'd first thought. Sometimes she even missed Menelaus, and she often felt guilty about leaving him.

Then the war had started. The dreadful, violent war. Hundreds of men had lost their lives, and all because of her. She'd begun to weave pictures into her wall hanging, showing scenes from the war – pictures of Greeks and Trojans fighting and killing each other.

Somehow, it made her feel better.

As she bent down to pick out a new spool of thread from her silver work basket, Andromache burst into the room. Her eyes were shining and she was clearly out of breath.

"I thought I'd find you here," she panted, glancing scornfully at the wall hanging. "Can't you find something more useful to do?"

Unlike her husband, Hector, Andromache wasn't very fond of Helen and blamed her for all Troy's troubles. Seeing Andromache always made Helen feel even more guilty. She knew Hector spent a lot more time on the battlefield than Paris did, even though it was Paris and Helen who'd caused the war.

"I have some news I think you should hear," continued Andromache.

Helen looked up.

"The men have been complaining to Hector, saying they're tired of fighting and asking him to do something about it. And he's so brave – do you know what he did? In the middle of a battle, he walked between the two armies, holding up his spear and shouting for silence. And they all went quiet and listened to him. Then he suggested to the Greek leaders that there should be a duel, and they've agreed to it!"

"A duel?" said Helen in surprise. "But who will he fight?"

"It won't be Hector fighting, you silly goose," said Andromache. "It'll be your darling Paris. And he'll be fighting Menelaus."

Helen felt a pang of guilt at the sound of her husband's name.

"But why?" she asked innocently, although of course, she knew. "Why are they fighting a duel?"

"Why do you think?" snapped Andromache. "To try to end the war, of course. And guess what prize the lucky winner gets?"

She paused and glanced mischievously at Helen.

"I . . . I don't know," said Helen, feeling flustered.

"He gets *you!*" crowed Andromache. "*You're* the prize!"

Blushing, Helen pretended to rummage in her basket again. She wished Andromache would just stop tormenting her like this. But to her despair, Andromache kept going.

"Both sides have agreed to stop fighting so the duel can take place," she said. "It's so exciting, don't you think? This is the first truce since the war began – *and* the first chance for peace."

"Does Paris want to fight a duel?" asked Helen.

"I don't think Hector gave him any choice!" laughed Andromache.

"When's it to be?"

"Any minute now," said Andromache as she left the room. "Priam's gone up to one of the towers to watch."

Helen hesitated for a few moments, then picked up her cloak and hurried out of the palace.

When she came to the wall, King Priam and some of the other old men were up on the tower, waiting for the duel to begin.

Helen rarely left the palace, and the men were surprised to see her climbing the steps towards them. As she approached, her lovely hair shimmered in the sunlight.

"Well," one old man remarked, "she really is a beauty – no wonder they're fighting over her."

"She's brought us nothing but trouble," his companion muttered.

Priam smiled. He knew that lots of his people hated Helen and blamed her for all the misery the war had caused, but he was fond of her.

"Helen, my dear," he called gently. "Have you heard? There's going to be a duel. They're preparing for it now."

Helen was trembling as Priam kindly took her arm.

"So it's true," she said, quietly. "I suppose it's a good thing if it helps to end the war, but. . . Oh, sometimes I wish Paris and I had never met!"

Priam had wished this himself many times, but he didn't want to hurt Helen's feelings. He just said, "Well, maybe this duel will settle things one way or another."

Helen looked the other way, hoping that Priam wouldn't see the tears in her eyes. How could she explain that, though she had run away from Menelaus, she couldn't bear the thought of Paris killing him? But neither did she have any wish to see Paris meet his death on the plain below. She couldn't bear the thought of either of them dying on her behalf. She felt terrible.

As she gazed down at the troops, she realized with a shock that she recognized some of the Greek soldiers. There was Ulysses! Helen remembered him as a young man – he'd been one of her admirers. And there was Agamemnon, her brother-in-law, the leader of the Greek army. Helen scanned the crowd anxiously for Menelaus, but couldn't spot him.

Suddenly a cry went up from the old men nearby.

"They're ready! The duel's about to begin!"

Helen couldn't stand this any more. Leaving them jostling for the best position on the wall, she slipped away and hurried back to the palace.

Meanwhile, down on the plain, Menelaus was eager to start fighting. He paced up and down impatiently while Hector and Ulysses measured out the ground. At last he had a chance to get his revenge on the man who had stolen his wife. Paris might be better-looking, but Menelaus was older, and the more experienced fighter. He'd survived similar duels in the past and knew what to expect: each man had just one chance with his spear. After that, it was down to a swordfight.

He glanced over to where his rival was waiting, surrounded by Trojan soldiers. As he watched, Paris took off his big bronze helmet, ran his fingers through his dark curls, then put the helmet on again.

Menelaus scowled in disgust and tightened his grip on his long, bronze-tipped spear. He could hardly wait to get his revenge.

"Everything's ready!" called Agamemnon. "We've drawn lots and Paris is to throw first."

Menelaus nodded. He took a deep breath and strode purposefully over to the position that had been marked for him. Paris took up his place opposite, and the rest of the soldiers stood some distance away, each army behind its own contestant.

Menelaus watched calmly as Paris prepared himself. Even though the younger man was to throw first, he was feeling confident. He trusted in his mighty shield, and in Paris's lack of skill.

In the distance, he saw the Trojan prince pace back a short way across the dusty ground. He took a run-up, and hurled the weapon with all his might. As it sailed through the sky, its long shadow shooting across the plain in his direction, Menelaus eyed it carefully. When it began to drop, he stepped forward and positioned his shield expertly.

Yes! Perfect! Paris's spear clattered noisily against the shield and bounced off to one side. A triumphant shout went up from the Greek army, and Menelaus's heart surged with pride and determination. Paris stared dejectedly at his wasted effort.

Menelaus now raised his own weapon above his shoulder. He took a step back.

Focusing hard on the small, distant figure of Paris, who was cowering behind his shield,

He cringed defensively as the Greek fighter slashed at him. . .

Menelaus summoned up every ounce of his strength and, with an almighty grunt of exertion, launched his spear into the blue air. It tore through the sky at terrifying speed, and the armies gasped as it plunged into Paris's shield.

The Trojan stumbled and fell, taking the full force of the blow. The crowd held its breath. Was he hurt? Menelaus waited.

Then, Paris got up.

"*Missed!*" said Menelaus angrily. As Paris tugged the spear out of his shield, everyone saw that his breastplate was torn on one side. He had escaped death by inches.

This only increased Menelaus's determination to finish his pathetic rival off once and for all. By rights, Paris should be dead already.

Menelaus wasted no time. "*DIE!*" he screamed, charging at his enemy with his sword drawn.

As he ran, he burned with deadly hatred for Paris. He thought of Helen in that traitor's arms. How he longed to get his revenge! The next few seconds were his chance. Nothing could stop him now.

Paris glanced quickly around the battlefield. For a moment he looked as if he was about to flee in terror.

But when he caught sight of his comrades' expectant faces, he stood his ground and drew his sword.

His legs trembled, and he cringed defensively as the Greek fighter slashed at him with his sword. Empowered by fury, Menelaus had the strength of a lion. He raised his gleaming blade and brought it crashing down onto Paris's helmet.

Paris staggered back, dropped his sword and fell to his knees.

Menelaus struck again.

"Aaargh!" moaned Paris in terror, covering his face with his hands.

Menelaus struck a third

45

time, desperately trying to knock the helmet from Paris's head; but with the third blow, his silver blade splintered and shattered.

Menelaus stared in utter confusion at the useless sword hilt left in his hand.

"Lord Zeus. . ." he muttered desperately. "Zeus, please help me!"

Meanwhile, Paris was struggling to stand up. But before he succeeded, Menelaus dropped the broken hilt and grabbed at Paris's helmet. Clenching his fist around the Trojan's horsehair crest, he dragged Paris down again, and began to haul him along the ground, heading for the Greek side of the field.

"Viper! *Wretch!* Treacherous COWARD!" Menelaus panted with each step as he heaved forward.

Paris choked and spluttered as the tough leather helmet strap dug into his throat. He tried to scream for help, but he could scarcely breathe. Menelaus tugged harder, deliberately strangling his victim. If he couldn't kill him any other way,. this, Menelaus decided, would have to do.

Paris struggled and thrashed his arms wildly. He was vaguely aware of rows of faces staring at him as he began to lose consciousness.

Menelaus looked down and saw Paris's handsome face turning purple. He felt the Trojan's body relax, and he knew his opponent would soon be dead.

Then, just as Paris was about to breathe his last, the helmet strap snapped. Menelaus lurched backward as the helmet came away in his hands. He stared at it, amazed. The thick leather strap was neatly severed.

Menelaus knew it was impossible that the strap had broken under Paris's weight. It was far too thick and strong. That Trojan must have a god on his side. He stared despairingly at the sky.

"Zeus," he whispered, "where *are* you? Athene, give me strength!"

At that moment, as Paris was staggering to his feet, Menelaus spotted a spear lying nearby. He darted over, picked it up, and whirled around to face his enemy.

Weaponless and utterly exhausted, Paris stood in the middle of the battleground, staring groggily at Menelaus. He was at point-blank range.

"*Now, Trojan prince,*" Menelaus growled under his breath. "This time I've got you, you miserable *traitor.*" And he hurled his spear, fast as a thunderbolt, straight as an arrow and with deadly accuracy, straight at Paris's heart.

"Duck!" shouted someone from the Trojan end.

But Paris was gone. Where he had been standing, there was nothing but a swirl of mist.

Hera and Athene were watching the action from the slopes of Mount Olympus. Athene was particularly enjoying herself – there was nothing she liked better than a good duel, and she knew Menelaus was going to win. She'd done enough to help him, after all – she'd guided his weapons, given him the idea of grabbing Paris's helmet, and helped him spot his spear again at the end. There was simply no competition. So when Paris disappeared, both goddesses were shocked.

"Hey, what's going on?" Athene complained, peering down at the scene. "Menelaus was meant to win!"

"Hmmm," said Hera, frowning. "I think I can guess what's happened. Follow me."

She led Athene up the mountainside until they reached the palace at the top. Once inside, Hera strode through the halls and passages, searching for her husband. Athene hurried along behind her, the crest on her helmet bobbing as she went.

They found Zeus sipping a cup of nectar beside a shady pool in the courtyard. Aphrodite was sitting at his feet, carefully inspecting her reflection in the clear water.

Hera marched up to them.

"I thought I'd find you here," she said, eyeing Aphrodite suspiciously. Aphrodite just smiled.

"Hera, my dear," said Zeus guiltily. "And Athene. I haven't seen either of you all day. Wherever have you been?"

"Watching the duel," replied Hera, glaring at him.

"Ah yes, the duel," said Zeus, avoiding her eyes.

"And we want to know what's going on," continued Hera.

Zeus scratched his beard and stole a nervous look at Aphrodite.

"I saw that meddling fool Thetis leaving the palace the other day. You're plotting something with her, aren't you?" said Hera. "It's no good trying to hide it – I can always tell when you're up to your tricks."

Aphrodite giggled.

"Oh, I'm sure you're involved too," snapped Hera. "You'd do anything to help that pretty Trojan prince of yours."

Aphrodite shrugged.

"All I did was make a little mist," she said innocently. "There's no harm in that, is there?"

Hera and Athene exchanged furious glances.

"I knew it!" exploded Hera. "So where have you hidden him?"

"He's safe in the city with Helen, where he belongs," laughed Aphrodite, twirling her finger around on the surface of the water.

"Don't you *realize* what you've

done?" fumed Athene, staring at her half-sister. "That would have been it – the whole war would have been over! The Greeks would have won! Now you've ruined everything!"

"I suppose *you* allowed her to interfere?" Hera hissed at Zeus. "Well, it's clear whose side you're on. So what happens now?"

Zeus hesitated, racking his brains to think of a solution that pleased everyone. He'd promised Thetis he would help the Trojans, but he could hardly pretend that Paris had won the duel when he'd disappeared before the end. He decided to try for a compromise.

"It seems to me," he began slowly, "that Menelaus has won the duel."

Athene smiled smugly.

"So my feeling is," Zeus went on, "that Helen should be returned to her husband and the Greeks should sail home. That way, the war will be over without Troy having to be destroyed."

"No!" shouted Aphrodite. "They can't give Helen back – she's Paris's wife now. They never *will* give her back, anyway!" she added childishly.

"Well then," bellowed Hera, "if the Trojans are going to be difficult, they deserve to be attacked."

"Hear, hear!" shouted Athene. "The Greeks will just have to destroy the city, won't they, if they can't get Helen any other way."

"Anyway," Aphrodite sulked, "Menelaus *didn't* win the duel – nobody won it."

"Exactly," said Hera, agreeing with Aphrodite for once. "Nobody won it. It was unfinished and there's no winner. The war must go on!"

Zeus sighed as he looked from one to the other.

"All right," he said at last. "The war will go on. Athene – can you make sure of that?"

"Of course, Father," replied the goddess of war, smiling triumphantly at Hera. "Just leave it to me."

Back on the plain, Menelaus was beside himself with rage.

"Coward!" he roared. "How typical of a Trojan to cheat his way out of things!"

"Calm down," Agamemnon said. "It's obvious that you've won the duel. As soon as I can find Hector, I'll speak to him about getting Helen back. Has anyone seen him?"

"I've sent Ajax to look for him," Ulysses reported.

"We'll wait forever if Ajax is looking – his brain's about the size of a berry," complained Menelaus. "If only Achilles were here. . . "

Agamemnon glared at him.

While the leaders were discussing the situation, the two armies were growing restless. The

Greeks were shouting for Paris to be brought back to finish the duel. The Trojans were jeering, claiming Paris had won by outwitting Menelaus.

They were all so busy hurling insults that no one noticed Athene appearing at the side of a Trojan soldier called Pandarus. She leaned forward, put her mouth very close to his ear and whispered something. Then she vanished.

Suddenly, Pandarus stepped out from the crowd with his bow and arrow. He drew back the bowstring, took aim and fired a shot straight at Menelaus.

A roar went up from the crowd. All at once, Menelaus clutched his waist and fell to his knees. He bravely grasped the arrow with both hands, and agonizingly twisted it out.

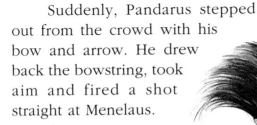

Agamemnon knelt down beside him. "Are you all right?" he asked anxiously.

"How deep is the wound?"

"Not too deep," gasped his brother, as a rivulet of blood trickled down his thigh. "I'll survive."

He winced in pain. "I'll need a doctor to stop the bleeding. . . but how could this happen?" he groaned in frustration. "We were so close. . ."

Ulysses immediately sent for a doctor, and Agamemnon got to his feet, seething with anger.

"I *thought* we agreed on a truce," he thundered. "Why should *we* keep to the ceasefire if the Trojans can't?"

"Maybe it was a mistake," said Ulysses. "Perhaps we shouldn't—"

"I don't care what it was," shouted the king. "It's clear they can't be trusted. Give the order – tell the troops that the truce is over. Let the fighting begin again!"

Chapter five

HECTOR RUNS RIOT

As dawn rose, Agamemnon lay tossing and turning in his bed. He'd been unable to sleep. For the last few days, the Trojans had been fighting fiercely. With each battle, they'd driven the Greek army back across the plain, away from the city and closer to the shore. Soon they'd be in a position to attack the camp and destroy the ships.

The Trojan leader, Hector, was the main problem now. Since Paris had failed in his own attempt to win the war, his older brother had returned to the fray with more strength than ever. The man was so brave – he didn't seem to fear anything. And he was as tall and powerful as Achilles himself.

Agamemnon felt ashamed. If only he hadn't offended Achilles!

But it was too late now. He turned over again and sighed.

The following afternoon, Hector leaned heavily against the gates of Troy, as the sun beat down remorselessly onto the plain.

His heart was pounding. Behind him he could hear men shouting and weapons clashing as the battle raged. He wiped away the beads of sweat that were trickling down the back of his neck. The fighting had started early that morning, and every muscle in Hector's body was worn out and aching. He badly needed a rest.

As he set off down the dusty streets inside the city, his sword swinging at his side, children stopped their games and turned to stare.

"Look! It's Hector," they whispered. And they picked up their toy swords and pretended to fight, dreaming of the day when they would be old enough to carry a real weapon into battle.

When he reached the palace, Hector headed for his wife's chamber.

"Andromache!" he called. "Are you there?"

Andromache appeared in the doorway, with their baby in her arms.

"Hector!" she said, relieved. "I

was just thinking about you."

Hector smiled and kissed her cheek. Then he bent down until his face was close to the child's. "And how's my little boy?" he murmured.

For a moment, the baby stared up in terror at the huge bronze helmet with its nodding plume of horsehair. Then he buried his face in his mother's dress and started to scream.

"Come on, Astyanax," Hector cooed gently. "Come to Daddy." But the baby went on wailing.

"It's that helmet!" declared Andromache. "Take it off, you'll scare him to death. And you've got blood all over you!"

"All right," said Hector, lifting the helmet from his head and placing it carefully on the ground. He took the baby in his arms and cuddled him. "But there is a war on, you know. I'll have to go back in a few minutes."

"Now don't go overdoing it, Hector," warned Andromache. "I know what you're like. This battle's been going on all day and you must be exhausted."

"But we're nearly there," Hector argued. "Just a couple more days and we can bring those Greeks to their knees. They haven't got Achilles, and if we really go for it now—"

He broke off. Andromache was looking at him sulkily.

"You always put the war first!" she complained. "What about us? Your wife and child?"

"Look, I have no choice," Hector pleaded. "They *need* me. It's not as if Paris is going to lead the troops, is it? I'm the only one who can do it. And we're so close to winning. When we've won, I'll spend more time with you – I promise."

"But *must* you go back immediately?" Andromache asked.

"You know I must," replied her husband. He passed the baby back to her. "And on my way I'm going to find that good-for-nothing brother of mine. We need everyone we can get – even Paris," he added, grimacing.

"I think he's with Helen," said Andromache. Hector laughed bitterly.

"Well, what a surprise!" he exclaimed. "Of course it's too much to expect him to leave his darling Helen!" Then his tone changed as he turned to his wife. "Pray for us, Andromache," he asked. "Pray to Zeus to let us win this war."

Andromache swallowed hard and smiled up at him.

"I will," she said, standing on tiptoe to kiss him goodbye.

Hector sighed and picked up his helmet. He strode along the passage that led to Helen's chamber. From the doorway, he saw his brother sprawling lazily on a couch. As Hector watched, Paris crammed a handful of grapes into his mouth.

The sticky juice dribbled down his chin and dripped onto the front of his tunic.

"I see you're much too busy to fight for your city," said Hector, walking in. "I'd have thought that the man who caused this war would be first on the battlefield."

Paris leaped to his feet, knocking the basket of grapes onto the floor.

"Hector!" he gasped. "I was just on my way." Hector snorted.

"How's the battle going?" asked Helen, who was sitting on a stool, busily spinning wool.

"All right, thanks," said Hector briskly. "But it would help if *all* our soldiers were fighting," he added, glaring angrily at his brother.

Paris was fumbling with the fastenings on his breastplate.

"You go on ahead," he said. "I'll catch up with you."

"No," Hector insisted sternly. "You'll come with me. *Now.*"

A few minutes later, Paris kissed Helen, slung his shield over his shoulder and grabbed his spear.

"I'm ready!" he announced.

"About time too," muttered Hector impatiently

That night, Agamemnon still couldn't sleep. It had been another bad day, and many Greeks had lost their lives. Agamemnon knew this couldn't go on – another few days like this one and they'd have no choice but to surrender – but what was the answer? They needed a plan, and fast.

He got up, slipped on his sandals and wrapped a fur cloak around his shoulders. As he stepped out of the tent, he shivered in the chilly night air. The stars were twinkling.

Agamemnon paced nervously around the silent camp, racking his brains. In the distance, he could just make out the guards' fires burning along the tops of the walls of Troy. Their lights flickered faintly in the darkness.

Then, as he gazed out across the plain, an idea suddenly came to him. He stood there for a few more moments, then he smiled to himself, turned and hurried back to his tent.

At first light, he called a meeting with the other leaders.

"I've had an idea," he said. The others looked at him expectantly.

"Well, the thing we want to avoid is the Trojans reaching the ships," he began. "Right?"

"Right," said Menelaus. "And?"

"And they're getting closer. So what I propose is, we build a wall."

"A wall?" said Ulysses, frowning.

"Yes!" Agamemnon excitedly. "A huge, strong wall between us and the Trojans, with battlements along the top, a ditch, gates, everything. Then they won't be able to get to the shore. If we start now, we could have it done in a day or so!"

"Is this really going to work?" Ulysses said, tentatively. "I mean,

wouldn't we be better coming up with a plan of attack?"

"Of course it'll work!" said Agamemnon. "Look, Ulysses, I'll put you in charge. Then you can make sure it works."

It didn't take Ulysses long to produce a plan for the wall. First they would dig a deep ditch. The soil from the ditch would be used to make a ridge, and the wall would go on top of that.

"How will *we* get through it?" asked Diomedes, examining the plan carefully.

"Well," said Ulysses, "There'll be gateways here, and here. And when we ride into battle, we'll go *around* the wall, at this end. We'll keep that area heavily guarded, of course. And the other end will be blocked by the sea. And," he added, "we'll put pointed stakes in the ditch, sticking out of the ground. They should be a strong enough deterrent."

Ulysses also worked out a system of shifts, so that some soldiers could work on the wall while others were fighting.

The first group of soldiers began their arduous task that morning. Half of them dug the ditch, while the other half piled up the soil to form the ridge. There was no shade on the plain and it was hot, sweaty work.

By midday, the ditch and the

ridge were finished. The exhausted soldiers trudged off to join the fighting and a second group took over. Again, they split into two teams – one gathering all the stones they could find, the other starting to build them into a wall. They fitted the stones together as closely as they could, then filled the gaps with soil. The sun beat down relentlessly as the wall rose higher and higher.

Whenever he saw the men beginning to tire, Ulysses moved among them, offering words of encouragement and helping with various tasks. By mid-afternoon the heat was worse than ever. Water was passed around in jars and the soldiers gulped it down greedily. Sweat and water mingled with dirt until their hands and faces were streaked with muddy smears.

When the wall had reached its full height, the last group of soldiers took their turn. They'd been fighting all day and were already worn out. One team built battlements along the top of the wall, so they'd be able to stand on the ridge and fire through the gaps at the Trojans on the other side. The other team lashed pieces of wood together to make the gates. Then they fitted these into the openings in the wall.

The sun was just starting to set when both teams joined together to work on the final task. They sharpened hundreds of wooden stakes and planted them firmly in the floor of the ditch, with their pointed ends facing up.

In the evening, when the day's fighting was over and the wall was complete, Agamemnon walked slowly along it, inspecting it carefully.

"A fine wall," he said, sounding impressed and clapping Ulysses on the back by way of thanks. But deep down, even Agamemnon felt slightly afraid.

"I hope it works," he said anxiously under his breath. "It's *got* to work."

And with that, he headed for his tent, hoping for some sleep at last.

The next day, Hector was sure, the Greeks would surrender. They were definitely fading fast – yesterday they'd had far fewer men than usual. Just one final push, and Hector was confident the Trojans would drive their opponents back to the shore.

Brandishing his spear, he ordered his driver to take him wherever the battle was fiercest. One minute, he was attacking savagely from his chariot; the next, he was fighting on foot. And as the day wore on, the Trojans forced the Greeks farther and farther back. Soon, they would be in sight of the ships.

Hector was on top of his chariot, about to urge his troops on with a rallying cry, when he saw something in the distance.

"What on earth is that?" he said.

It was a flag. A bold, bright battle flag, fluttering in the wind.

"What's it doing up there?" said Hector. The flag was far too high up to be on top of a chariot. Then, as Hector peered through the forest of spears, horses and chariots ahead of him, he began to make out the shape of the wall looming in the distance.

"Those shifty Greek cowards!" he cursed, staring at the broad, imposing structure. "Pathetic *cheats!* That does it!" he shouted. "If they think a pile of earth and stones

is going to stop ME, they're WRONG!" And he urged his soldiers onward, storming ahead into the thick of battle more determinedly than ever.

Meanwhile, Agamemnon was trying to rally his troops. He caught sight of Diomedes tearing past in his chariot, and bellowed at him.

"Get to the front and keep attacking. Don't let them think we've given up. We *must* force them back!"

Raising his arm in acknowledgement, Diomedes disappeared into the fray. As Agamemnon turned to tell his driver which way to go, he found himself almost face to face with a young Trojan soldier. And before the Greek leader could raise his weapon, the boy lunged forward with his spear. For an instant, Agamemnon was aware of an excruciating pain shooting up his arm. Then he slipped into unconsciousness.

When he awoke, he was back at the camp. At first, he couldn't remember what had happened. He tried to sit up, but the pain in his arm forced him to lie down again on the couch.

"Is anybody there?" he shouted.

The army doctor hurried into the tent, accompanied by Briseis – the servant girl Agamemnon had stolen from Achilles.

"Now, now, sir," said the doctor. "You mustn't get excited. You have a nasty wound on your arm and you've been asleep for several hours."

"Several hours!" exploded the king. "But what about the battle? What's going on? Are we winning?"

"Things aren't looking good, sir," replied the doctor, while Briseis tried to persuade Agamemnon to sip some water. "Menelaus is still on the field – and Ajax too. But we've lost a lot of men, and many more are wounded."

Agamemnon sighed in despair and pushed the cup away. "What about Ulysses?" he asked, half afraid to hear the answer. "And Diomedes?"

"Both wounded, sir. They've had to withdraw. Ulysses has been stabbed in the ribs and Diomedes was shot in the foot – by one of Paris's arrows, I'm told."

Agamemnon covered his face with the sheet. He couldn't bear to hear any more.

The plain was a seething mass of horses, chariots and foot soldiers, and the noise was deafening. The air was so thick with the dust kicked up by the horses' thundering hoofs that the men could hardly breathe. Bodies littered the ground.

Hector spurred his men on, fighting boldly with those at the front, then racing back to encourage those at the rear.

Ajax, the strongest Greek left on the field, fought valiantly, doing his best to keep the Trojans back. But one by one, the Greek soldiers fell and the Trojans inched forward across the plain, until the battle was raging right in front of the ditch.

Hector fought like a whirlwind, and as they chased the last of the Greeks back through the wall gates, he roared at his men to cross the ditch. It was too wide for the horses to jump, so the Trojans abandoned their chariots and leaped in on foot. They tried to avoid the sharp stakes, but many Trojan soldiers were impaled on the spikes and hung there in agony, bleeding to death. The rest scrambled out on the other side of the ditch and scrambled up the ridge, heading for the wall itself.

Ajax, the strongest Greek left on the field, fought valiantly

The Greeks hurried up onto the battlements and began hurling stones and firing arrows down on the Trojan troops, who were attempting to dismantle the wall from below. Wrenching stones from it wherever they could, they tried to tear it down. But the wall was too strong and thick. However much rock and soil they pulled out of it, it stood firm.

"The gates!" screamed Hector, weaving through the stakes at the bottom of the ditch. "Attack the weakest point!" The Trojan soldiers charged along the ridge, congregating at the central gate. Hundreds of them were pounding on it with spears, swords, stones – even their bare hands.

As soon as Hector reached the gate, he snatched up a huge rock that was lying at his feet. Groaning, he lifted it above his head and, with an almighty yell, smashed it with full force against the gate. The carefully built wooden door splintered from top to bottom. Tearing away the fractured pieces, Hector made an opening large enough to step through.

Seconds later, the Greeks were horrified to see Hector appearing on the other side of the wall, his spear in his hand and his eyes flashing wildly.

"To the ships!" he roared. "Let's burn them!"

And as the Trojan army swarmed through the hole behind him, the Greeks fled in terror back to their camp.

Hera was sitting on her golden throne in Zeus's palace, fuming with rage. The Trojans were winning the war and it was all because that silly busybody Thetis had sneaked off to Zeus and cajoled him into helping her. And of course, Zeus was so weak, he couldn't say no.

Well, she'd show him!

She strode along to her chamber, locked the door and set to work. First, she had a long bath. She scrubbed her skin until it was spotlessly clean. Then she rubbed scented oil all over her body, from head to toe. She rummaged through her wardrobe and pulled out her most beautiful dress – Athene had made it for her and had painstakingly embroidered it with hundreds of peacocks. When she'd fastened the dress with a golden brooch at her throat, she tied a shimmering sash around her waist. Finally, she combed out her long, dark hair and pinned it up on her head in a cascade of curls.

When she was ready, she put on her best sandals and hurried to the kitchen. Pleased to find that there was no one there, she quickly filled a basket with a loaf of freshly-baked barley bread, a lump of goat's cheese, some figs, a pot of honey and a large flask of wine. Then she slipped out of the palace.

She made her way down the mountainside until she reached a small cave. She listened for a moment outside, then bent down and stepped through the entrance.

"Sleep!" she called into the pitch darkness. "Are you there?"

There was a rustling, followed by a very loud yawn. Then a drowsy voice said, "Who is it? Who's there?"

"It's Queen Hera. Wake up immediately – I need your help."

Sleep sighed. Then Hera heard him get out of bed and stumble across the cave. A soft light appeared, and Sleep stood there in his nightgown, holding a lamp in one hand and rubbing his eyes with the other.

"What can I do for you, Madam?" he asked, stifling another yawn.

Hera went up to him and whispered something in his ear. He nodded sleepily and shuffled slowly over to an old wooden chest at the back of the cave. After a lot of rummaging around, he pulled out a tiny silver bottle.

"Now, you won't use too much, will you?" he asked dreamily, handing it to Hera.

"I'll use just as much as I need," she said brightly, popping the bottle into her basket and heading for the entrance. "Thank you. And goodbye."

"Goodbye," mumbled Sleep,

who was already halfway back to bed. As Hera stepped out into the sunlight, she heard the sound of heavy snoring.

A little way down the mountainside, Hera found Zeus sitting under an oak tree.

"Hera, my dear!" he exclaimed in surprise. "How very beautiful you're looking today."

"I thought we could take a walk together through the forest," said Hera, flashing him what she hoped was a charming smile.

"What a splendid idea," said Zeus, scrambling to his feet and brushing leaves from his tunic.

"I've brought some food," said Hera, pointing to the basket.

"Even better!" laughed Zeus. "Off we go then."

They walked hand in hand through the forest, talking, laughing and stopping to look at unusual birds. Zeus couldn't help wondering why his wife was being so nice to him. Still, it made a pleasant change from her usual bad temper. And she looked and smelled divine.

After a while, they sat down in a sunny clearing that was carpeted with yellow crocuses and hyacinths. Hera spread the food out on a cloth and Zeus ate as much as he could. He also drank a lot of wine, and soon felt very tired. Lying down on the soft grass, he fell fast asleep.

Hera waited a few minutes. Then she reached into the basket and brought out the silver bottle. She pulled out the stopper, tipped up the bottle and sprinkled the contents onto Zeus's face. The sparkling droplets were as clear as raindrops. Zeus twitched his nose, but didn't wake. When the bottle was empty, Hera packed the remains of the meal into the basket and crept away.

As soon as she arrived back at the palace, she went to find Athene. "I need your help," she said.

Athene looked up from polishing her spear.

"I've put Zeus to sleep for a while, and I want you to help the Greek army," continued Hera. "Those Trojans are doing far too well."

Athene was always pleased to get involved in a war, so she flew down to where the battle was still raging. Hector had fought his way close to the ships and the Greeks had almost given up hope. The goddess made herself invisible and flitted from one soldier to another, whispering words of encouragement in their ears.

With a sudden burst of energy, the Greek army started to fight back. Hector threw a spear at Ajax, which hit his shield and bounced away. A few minutes earlier, Ajax would have sighed with relief and pulled his shield closer to his body. But now, he picked up a large rock and hurled it straight at Hector's head. It hit him right on the throat, making him topple back a little. He staggered around in a daze for a few minutes, clutching his neck. Then he dropped to the dusty ground.

Shouting triumphantly, the Greeks surged forward. The Trojans rushed to protect their leader. They fought off the worst of the attack, then carried him to safety, back to his chariot on the other side of the ditch. They lifted him in, and the driver ordered the horses to trot. The rattling chariot jolted Hector's wounded body. Within seconds, he had fainted from the pain.

Zeus drifted slowly back to consciousness. For a moment, he

wondered where he was. Then he remembered the walk and the picnic, and felt very suspicious. Hera was up to something and he was sure it involved the war.

Struggling to his feet, he rubbed his eyes and looked down on the battle. He was shocked at what he saw. The Greeks had forced the Trojans back behind the wall and across the ditch. Athene was on the battlefield, helping the Greeks. And Hector, amazingly, was unconscious and on his way back to Troy.

Guessing immediately that he'd been tricked, Zeus stormed back to the palace in a furious temper. He searched high and low for Hera but she was nowhere to be found.

"Hermes!" he bellowed. "Come here now!"

Hermes appeared instantly.

"Yes, Father?" he said.

"Go to the battlefield and tell Athene to keep out of this war. Tell her to come back here this minute."

"Yes, Father," said Hermes, turning to leave.

"Wait!" shouted Zeus. "I haven't finished yet. On your way, find Apollo and tell him to come and see me at once."

Hermes scurried off, and a few minutes later, Apollo sauntered in.

"Hermes said you wanted to see me, Father," he said.

"Yes," said Zeus. "I want you to go down to Troy, stop Hector's chariot and make sure he gets back to the battle as soon as possible."

"I'll do my best, Father," said Apollo casually.

"You'll do what I say!" roared Zeus. "And jump to it!"

"Yes, Father," muttered Apollo. And he disappeared.

A short while later, Hector was fully recovered and fighting more fiercely than ever. The Greeks were shocked to see him – they'd hoped he was dead. And without Athene's help, they were in trouble again.

"This war's not over yet!" said Zeus, looking down at the Trojans advancing over the plain, across the ditch and back through the gate. Once more, the battle raged dangerously close to the shore.

At last, Hector reached one of the ships. He tried to climb onto it, but Ajax was quicker and leaped up first. He desperately fought Hector off with his sword, as the Trojan leader grabbed at the ship's sides.

"Bring me fire!" shouted Hector to the men nearest him. "Bring me fire to burn the ships!"

Zeus sighed with satisfaction.

"What a good thing I woke up when I did," he said to himself. "Just wait till I find that wife of mine. . . ."

Chapter six

BRAVE PATROCLUS

When Achilles had withdrawn from the war, he had moved his men along the coast, away from the main camp. And now all was quiet around his tent, except for the sound of waves lapping gently on the shore.

Pairs of horses stood beside their chariots, chomping the clover and parsley that grew on the damp ground. The men were chatting idly or training for battle with their spears and bows.

They had obeyed their leader's orders to leave the battle, but many of them felt frustrated and longed to rejoin the fighting. There was a feeling of restlessness in the air.

Inside the tent, Achilles was sitting on a stool, strumming his lyre. Patroclus, his closest comrade, was slicing up a leg of lamb, which he then threaded onto spits. He was about to place them over the fire to roast when he heard voices outside.

"Achilles!" called a herald's voice. "Ulysses is here to see you."

Achilles leaped to his feet and strode over to the doorway.

"Well, well," he exclaimed. "Visitors! Come on in." And in walked Ulysses with two heralds.

"Please, sit down," said Achilles. "Patroclus, cut some more meat and pour some wine for our guests. It's a long time since we've entertained anyone in this tent!"

"Achilles, I'll come straight to the point. I have a message for you," said Ulysses, lowering himself gently onto a couch and wincing slightly at the pain from his injured rib. "From Agamemnon."

Achilles smiled and said nothing.

"He wants you to return to the fighting."

Achilles remained silent.

"He's desperate, Achilles. So desperate, he's even talking about giving up and sailing home. I don't know if you've heard – Hector's reached the ships. . ."

Achilles's smile faded.

". . . and he's started setting fire

to them. Ajax is trying to fight him off, but we're in terrible trouble. So many of us are wounded and those that aren't are exhausted. You're our only hope."

There was a long pause. The only sound was the meat spitting and crackling on the fire.

Then Achilles spoke.

"I gave everything to his precious war for years – and what thanks did I get? He's treated me shamefully and I can't forgive him."

"He's willing to return the girl to you," said Ulysses.

"Now that he's desperate!" laughed Achilles.

"And anything else you want," Ulysses added hastily. "Gold, horses. . . please Achilles. I'm begging you! If not for Agamemnon's sake, then for the army's."

Again, there was silence. Patroclus sprinkled salt onto the meat and heaped it onto the plates. A servant girl brought in baskets of freshly-baked bread.

At last, Achilles said, "You can tell Agamemnon that I will return to the fighting. . . "

Ulysses held his breath and Patroclus glanced up.

". . . when Hector reaches *my*

ships, and not before. Now, let's eat while the food is hot."

Some time later, when the meal was over and the guests had gone, Patroclus was left alone in the tent. As he cleared away the plates and leftover food, his eye fell upon a pile of shiny objects on the floor – Achilles's huge sword, his helmet and his shield. He stared at them for a while. And suddenly, an idea came into his mind.

The battle was still raging near the ships on the other side of the camp. Ajax was worn out. His shoulder ached from the weight of his shield, his breath came in painful gasps and sweat soaked his tunic. One minute he'd been standing on the deck brandishing his sword, the next he was leaping to the ground empty-handed – the sword had been knocked from his grasp by Hector's own weapon.

Waves of utter despair swept over Ajax. What hope was there of victory now? The Trojans were advancing in their hundreds, spurred on by the sight of the spreading flames. Ajax had fought as hard as he could to keep the enemy away from the ships, but he'd failed. He could only watch helplessly as Hector raised his clenched fist in an arrogant gesture of triumph against a fiery backdrop of burning masts and sails.

Suddenly, a distant movement caught his eye. He glanced over to the far end of the beach and could hardly believe what he saw. A splendid chariot, pulled by two beautiful horses, was thundering along the shore! And behind it charged hundreds of soldiers. As the procession sped closer, Ajax shouted to Menelaus who was fighting nearby.

"Look! Over there!"

Menelaus turned to look, and his jaw fell open in amazement. There was no mistaking the golden horses tossing their shimmering manes. Their names were Xanthus and Balius – and everyone knew who they belonged to.

"Achilles," breathed Menelaus.

One after another, the Greek soldiers spotted the approaching horde. Slowly their astonishment turned to relief, and then to joy. Achilles had come to save them!

The new arrivals galloped into the fray and joined in the fighting immediately, their shiny bronze breastplates conspicuous among the blood-spattered ones all around. Meanwhile, Ajax was staring hard at their leader.

Achilles must have lost weight during his time away from the action. His usually tall, sturdy frame looked more slender, and his helmet seemed slightly loose. And there was something different about the way he was standing. . .

Then Ajax guessed the truth.

"It's not Achilles!" he muttered to himself. "It's Patroclus!"

By the time the other soldiers realized this, Patroclus and his men had managed to put out the fires on the ships. The latest recruits were

Hector raised his clenched fist in an arrogant gesture of triumph

bursting with energy and some of their enthusiasm rubbed off on their weary comrades. Patroclus himself was like a man inspired. Waving Achilles's silver-hilted sword above his head, he swept through the ranks, shouting orders to his driver, Automedon.

"Left, left! Quickly – over there! Now right – turn the horses right. No – *sharp* right!"

As the Greeks forced the Trojans to retreat, away from the shore and back to the wall, Patroclus remembered what Achilles had said after he'd given him permission to go.

"Just drive them away from the ships – don't try to take the city. You'll never succeed."

"If only I could, though. . ." thought Patroclus to himself. "If only I could lead the army to victory and march through Troy in triumph. Achilles would be so proud of me – I *know* he would."

Meanwhile, Hector was in trouble. At first, he'd tried to stand his ground, urging his men to do the same. But as he watched them being gradually swept back, defeat written all over their tired faces, he began to lose confidence. Though he kept battling away, the Greek spears and arrows seemed to be whistling through the air more quickly than before and he found himself being beaten back until he was right under the wall.

Leaning against the ridge for a moment, to catch his breath, he heard Paris shouting.

"Hector! Look out!"

Hector spun around to see a Greek archer aiming an arrow accurately at his head. Crouching, Hector scrambled up the ridge and through a gate, and just managed to throw himself behind the wall as the arrow zipped past him.

He paused for a moment, panting loudly. Then, glancing across to the other side of the ditch, he caught sight of his chariot and horses still standing there. Suddenly, he wanted nothing more than to return to safety. He had been a match for every man on the field. But Achilles was a different matter.

It took some time to get across. Hector had to pick his way carefully around the sharp stakes that protruded from the floor, treading awkwardly on the mangled bodies of men and horses. At last, he climbed up the other side. Weapons were raining down on him. Ducking behind his shield, he made a run for the chariot, leaped in and shouted at the driver.

"Head for the city!"

The driver hesitated, unable to

believe Hector was aban oning his men. Then he picked up the reins and urged the horses to gallop.

At that moment, Patroclus reached the wall. Through the open gate, he caught a glimpse of Hector's chariot disappearing into the distance. Snatching the reins from Automedon, he guided the nimble horses up the slope of the ridge and through the gateway. Then, to the amazement of the soldiers nearby, they leaped over the ditch, pulling the chariot behind them, and landed safely on the other side – a distance no ordinary horses could ever have

jumped. And they galloped off across the plain, in pursuit of Hector.

From high up on Olympus, Zeus was still keeping a sharp eye on the battle. When he saw Hector fleeing, he summoned Apollo and sent him down to the plain. Apollo quickly made himself invisible, slipped into the chariot beside Hector and whispered in his ear.

The closer Hector came to the city walls, the more he began to have second thoughts about what he was doing. He imagined his father's

disappointed face when he admitted that he'd run away. And he could almost hear the whispers that would spread around the city. . .

"Hector's a coward!"

"Calls himself a hero!"

"Not much of a leader!"

"Whoa!" he shouted suddenly, grabbing the reins from his driver, and hauling the horses to a stop. Then he turned the chariot, so that it once more faced the Greek army.

Patroclus was amazed to see the Trojan leader turn around again. Undeterred, he spurred on his team to gallop even faster. When his opponent's chariot was not far away, he pulled hard on the reins to slow the horses. Then, his heart pounding with fear and excitement, he sprang to the ground and, with all his strength, hurled his spear at Hector.

Patroclus's aim was good, and the weapon tore through the air towards the Trojan chariot. Hector darted to one side to avoid it, but his driver was not so quick. The spear's bronze tip struck him in the neck with full force, knocking him head-over-heels out of the chariot and onto the dusty ground.

Hector realized immediately that the man was dead.

The first thing Hector felt was a jolt of fear. For a moment, he hesitated. Then Apollo whispered in his ear once again, and he began to burn with fury. Tossing the reins aside, he took his sword, sprang from the chariot and charged at Patroclus.

Patroclus bravely stood his ground, trying to control his nerves. The Trojan leader was a fearsome sight, with his helmet plumes trailing behind him and his huge shield glinting in the evening sun.

"Stay calm, stay calm," muttered Patroclus, desperately attempting to prepare himself.

Hector thundered nearer. As soon as he came within striking distance, Patroclus instinctively raised his sword. But before he could bring it slicing down through the air, Hector lifted his own weapon and, in one swift movement, knocked Patroclus's helmet right off his head.

Patroclus watched in horror as the helmet fell with a heavy thud and rolled a little way before coming to a standstill under the horses' feet. Hector's piercing eyes gleamed menacingly through the eye-slits in his helmet as he moved closer. Patroclus could even hear the rasping sound of his breathing.

Terrified, he looked from left to right, in the hope that help was nearby, but he was alone. He tried to pull his shield closer to his body

Gripped by panic, he turned and ran

but his hands were wet with sweat. The shield slipped from his grasp and fell to the ground.

With neither helmet nor shield, Patroclus knew he had no chance. Gripped by panic, he turned and ran.

But he hadn't taken more than a few steps when his arm was seized in a vice-like grip. Struggling frantically, he tried to wrench himself free. Then he felt a sharp stab of pain, and a wave of dizziness swept over him. He looked down and, through an unfocused blur, saw the glint of silver, laced with his own red blood.

Then Patroclus slumped limply to the ground.

For a few seconds he lay there, concentrating on each breath. He tried to call out, but he had no voice left.

"Help me!" he croaked hoarsely. "Please, somebody – help me!"

But there was no one to hear him – no one but Hector. The last thought

Patroclus had was that he had failed Achilles. Then, he knew no more.

Ajax was still fighting. Pausing for a minute to wipe the sweat from his brow, he glanced across the plain. What he saw filled him with horror. Achilles's horses were running at full speed, out of control. There was no sign of Patroclus – only Automedon clinging to the reins.

And in the middle of the plain stood Hector, bending over a lifeless figure. As Ajax watched, the Trojan warrior forced his victim's sword out of his fingers, and picked up the helmet that lay nearby. Standing upright, Hector raised the sword triumphantly aloft in one hand, and the helmet in the other. And although he was some distance away, Ajax was almost certain that he was laughing.

Chapter seven

REVENGE!

Hephaestus, the blacksmith of the gods, was working away at his forge on Mount Olympus. He was wearing nothing but a loincloth, and as he pumped his bellows to fan the flames, the sweat trickled down his hairy chest. He paused for a minute to wipe his face and body with a sponge. Just as he was about to start beating a small piece of silver into shape on his anvil, he heard a knock at the big bronze door.

"Come in," he called.

The door swung open, and Thetis peeped in.

"Hello, Hephaestus," she said. "Are you very busy?"

"I'm never too busy for you, Thetis," smiled the smith, hobbling over to greet her. Many of the gods and goddesses teased Hephaestus because of his limp, but not Thetis. "Come and sit down."

He took her by the hand, led her over to the coolest part of the room and sat her down on a beautiful silver chair. Lowering himself onto a

matching footstool, he picked up his tunic from where it lay crumpled on the floor and pulled it over his head.

"How can I help you?" he asked.

Thetis glanced nervously at him and he noticed for the first time the tear stains on her cheeks.

"It's Achilles," she wailed. "He's in a terrible state, Hephaestus. I've never seen him like this before."

"Whatever's happened?" asked Hephaestus.

"Well," Thetis explained, "Patroclus persuaded Achilles to let him go into battle, and now he's dead – killed by Hector. Achilles is furious – furious with Hector for killing his friend, and with himself for letting Patroclus fight. Now he wants to rejoin the battle to take revenge on Hector. And I want to help him."

Hephaestus looked confused.

"Yes, yes, I know I wanted the Trojans to win," said Thetis uncomfortably, "but I – well, I've changed my mind. For Achilles's sake. The thing is," she went on, "he lent his helmet, sword and shield to Patroclus, and Hector's stolen them. So I was wondering. . . "

"If I'd make new ones for him?" smiled Hephaestus.

Thetis nodded.

"It would be a pleasure."

"I need them by dawn," said Thetis anxiously.

"Don't you worry," said the smith kindly, getting to his feet.

Hephaestus made his way back over to the furnace, pulling off his tunic as he went and tossing it aside. He picked up his bellows and fanned the flames until they flared up fiercely. Then he threw pieces of shining metal onto the fire – first gold, then silver, then bronze. While he waited for them to soften, he fumbled in his silver toolbox for his best hammer and tongs.

Early the next day, Agamemnon went to find Menelaus.

"You look exhausted!" said his brother, as Agamemnon trudged into the tent and sat down heavily.

"I haven't been sleeping," Agamemnon grunted. "My arm's still in agony. And how can I sleep when the army's on the verge of defeat? What are we going to do, Menelaus?"

Menelaus stared at the ground.

"If we have another day like yesterday, it will finish us," continued Agamemnon. "We need to come up with another plan."

"I don't know," Menelaus said. "The men are worn out – they can't keep Hector away from the ships forever. If *only* I'd won the duel," he said frustratedly. "We'd be on our way home now, and I'd have Helen back. . . " He trailed off sadly.

Agamemnon changed the subject. "What news of Patroclus?" he asked. Menelaus sighed.

"Ajax managed to drag his body off the battlefield last night," he said. "His breastplate was gone, and his helmet, everything. They carried him to Achilles's tent, and they've been up all night mourning him. Terrible business," Menelaus reflected.

"Well I hope the great Achilles is feeling guilty today," snarled Agamemnon.

Then he saw Menelaus's expression suddenly change. "What is it?" he said. "What's the matter?"

Menelaus had a clear view of the entrance. He was staring, transfixed, no longer seeming to hear a word his brother was saying. Agamemnon turned to look behind him.

There, standing in the doorway, was Achilles himself. On his head was a huge shining helmet, crowned by a rippling crest of golden horsehair. A mighty bronze sword, its silver hilt studded with gold, hung from his waist, and on his arm he carried an enormous shield, newly riveted and polished until it gleamed like a mirror.

Gold, silver and bronze sparkled in the lamplight, casting swirling reflections onto the sides of the tent.

Achilles said nothing. But his eyes were glinting with determination.

In the end it was Menelaus who broke the silence.

"Achilles!" he said at last, striding over and warmly shaking the warrior's free hand. "Welcome back!"

Agamemnon was more reserved. He stood up and eyed the armed man carefully.

"So, Achilles," he said "you're ready to fight, are you?"

"Yes, sir," replied Achilles. "I'm ready."

The battle was raging on the plain. The pattern of the previous day began to repeat itself as the Trojans forced the Greeks closer and closer to the wall.

Hector was physically tired but brimming with confidence. He was wearing the breastplate and helmet that he had taken from Patroclus and was determined that, today, he'd fight his way to the ships again and burn every single one. He spotted Paris nearby and beckoned him over to his chariot.

"I don't want you sneaking off back to the city today," he said sternly.

"Of course not," said Paris. Then he added, "We're doing well, aren't we?"

We need to do better if we're going to burn the ships. I want every man to be— "

"What's that?" interrupted Paris.

"What?" said Hector irritably. Why would Paris never concentrate on the task in hand?

"Over there – near the wall," continued Paris. "It looks like. . . it *is*. . . it's Achilles's chariot again!"

"Well I wonder who's in it today," said Hector. And the same thought struck them both. They glanced at each other, then stared across to where the golden horses were darting in and out of the battle.

"It can't be. . . " murmured Paris. "I thought he was dead!"

Hector screwed up his eyes trying to get a better view. There was the driver, Automedon. But who was standing behind him? Whoever it was, he was wearing a splendid helmet and holding the biggest shield Hector had ever seen.

"Surely it can't be. . . " He couldn't bring himself to say the name aloud. But the longer he watched, the more uneasy he felt.

The unknown soldier was tall, strong and broad-shouldered. He had a commanding air about him. He was wielding his sword with great skill, leaning out of the moving chariot to strike at anyone within reach. Soldiers were dropping to the ground all around him and Hector realized, to his horror, that the Trojan army was on the retreat, beaten back

across the plain by the new arrival.

"It *is* him," muttered Hector. His earlier confidence began to drain away and he shot an anxious glance at Paris. "It's *Achilles*. . . "

"Hector, look!" shouted Paris suddenly. "Isn't that Polydorus?"

Polydorus was Priam's youngest son. Over the last few weeks, he'd been begging his parents to let him join the fighting. But Priam had insisted he wasn't yet old enough to get involved in the deadly battles.

Now it seemed that the boy had disobeyed his father. He shouldn't even have been outside the city, but his two brothers, watching in horror, saw him ride his horse right up to Achilles's chariot. Inexperienced as he was, Polydorus approached from the front, giving Achilles plenty of warning. He raised his spear and aimed at his opponent's head, but Achilles leaned expertly to one side, and the spear flew past him.

Immediately, Achilles drew back his own spear to retaliate. Stricken with fear, Polydorus tried to turn his horse and ride away, but he was too slow. Achilles's spear shot through the air and tore into the middle of his back, knocking him sprawling from his horse.

Polydorus was dead.

Hector realized, to his horror, that the Trojan army was on the retreat

Paris gasped and turned to his brother, but Hector had gone. He was already charging across the plain, heading for Achilles and vowing to avenge his brother. When he was within striking distance, he hurled his spear with all the force he could muster, aiming for Achilles's back. But the gods were still watching from Mount Olympus, and Athene quickly blew on the spear as hard as she could. It curved around in a wide arc until it was facing the opposite direction. Then it landed gently on the ground.

At that moment, Achilles turned and saw Hector. The anger he already felt for the man who had killed his best friend turned to wild fury when he saw that the Trojan leader was wearing *his* helmet.

"Arrogant fool! How *dare* he!" he spat from between clenched teeth. Then he shouted, "Get me my spear!"

One of the nearby foot soldiers ran to where Polydorus's body lay on the ground. He dragged the spear out, and delivered it to its owner.

"Charge!" yelled Achilles. And Xanthus and Balius, his magical golden horses, sprang into action.

Raising his arm as the chariot hurtled forward, Achilles let out a terrifying roar. He was just about to throw his spear, when, all of a sudden, a heavy mist fell in front of him, shrouding Hector from view.

On Mount Olympus, Apollo smiled a satisfied smile.

Confused, Achilles lowered his arm and peered intensely into the swirling whiteness. The Trojan leader had vanished from sight! Achilles was furious. He paused for a moment, then shouted into the void.

"I'll be back, Hector! You can hide yourself away in the mist but I'll get you in the end!"

Then he wheeled his chariot around and headed back into the thick of the battle. Spurred on by rage, he fought like a madman throughout the day. He killed dozens of soldiers, while his horses trampled over the bodies already scattered across the ground. And as more and more blood spattered the sides of his chariot, the Trojans began to flee back to the city.

King Priam and Queen Hecuba were watching from the city wall, but they couldn't see the other side of the battlefield. When they saw the Trojan army fleeing across the plain, Priam called out to a messenger.

"What's happening? Why are our men retreating?"

"It's Achilles!" panted the man. "He's back! He's slaughtering us, your majesty – the men just can't

stand up to him. And it looks as if he won't stop until he finds Hector."

Priam looked at his wife. Hecuba was wringing her hands and staring desperately out at the plain.

"Priam," she said at last, turning to him with tears in her eyes. "Please put a stop to this. Let the army back inside the gates – just for a while. Just so they can recover their strength."

Priam squeezed her hands tightly. "The Greeks will think we've surrendered if I do that," he said.

"But Priam, Hector's out there. And Paris. . ." The queen's tears welled up and she began to sob against his shoulder.

Priam knew she was right. It was too dangerous. With one last glance out over the plain, the king made his way down the steps to the gateway below. The guards leaped to their feet.

"Who's in charge here?" Priam demanded.

A burly, bearded man stepped forward.

"I am, sir."

"Open the gates," Priam ordered.

There was silence. The guard stared at the king in disbelief.

"But, sir—" he protested.

"Do as I say," said Priam. "Now."

The king climbed back up to the wall and took his wife's arm, as the grating sound of the bars being pulled back echoed up the stone steps. Then, while the king and queen watched their army coming closer and closer, with the Greeks in pursuit, the huge gates were dragged open below them.

The exhausted soldiers began streaming through the gate. They swarmed into the city in their hundreds, heading straight for the wells – they were desperate to drink. Slumping to the ground, they gulped down the water and wiped the sweat and dust from their filthy bodies.

Among the first to enter the city was Paris. When Hector had headed off to attack Achilles, Paris had stayed skulking as near to the gates as possible. He joined his parents on the wall, but when he saw his mother rushing joyfully over to embrace him, he realized they knew nothing about what had happened to Polydorus. Trembling, he took a deep breath, preparing to break the grim news.

A while later, Hector rode close to the wall in his chariot.

"What's going on?" he yelled. How can I fight a war without any soldiers? Close the gates again!"

"No, Hector," Priam shouted back. "The men must come in for a rest. I can't let them all die."

"Hector!" wailed Hecuba with tears streaming down her face. "Come inside!"

"Achilles is coming!" shouted Paris. Peering at the horizon, he had spotted the Greek's chariot heading for the city. "Get *in*, while you still can!"

"I'll go and ward him off!" Hector yelled up at them. And before his distraught mother could say anything, he had wheeled his horses around and set off across the plain.

The last of the Trojan soldiers were surging through the gates, the Greeks still hot on their heels. Priam scanned the plain desperately, but Hector was nowhere to be seen.

"We must close the gates to stop the Greeks from getting in," he said.

"No!" gasped Hecuba. "We can't leave our own son outside to face Achilles alone."

"We can't risk Achilles getting into the city," said Priam, and he hurried down the steps.

"Close the gates!" he called to the guards.

"Priam!" screamed Hecuba from above. "*No!*"

The guards hesitated.

"Close them!" ordered the king.

Slowly, the heavy wooden gates were heaved shut, and the bars were drawn firmly across.

Achilles steadied himself as his chariot rumbled at breakneck speed closer and closer to the city gates. As he drew near to the gleaming

79

walls of Troy, he saw that only Greek soldiers remained outside. Those cowardly Trojans had all run for cover!

Greek breastplates, Greek swords and helmets adorned the soldiers who jostled around the enemy gates.

·Achilles slowed his chariot.

Then he saw him. A tall, burly soldier, standing a little way along the walls, next to a battered Trojan chariot. No wonder he hadn't recognized this Trojan warrior at first sight. For he too was wearing a Greek helmet and a Greek breastplate – Achilles's own.

It was Hector.

"MURDERER!" yelled Achilles, clutching his sword and springing down from the chariot. The hordes of Greek warriors made way for Achilles as he headed relentlessly for his enemy, storming across the plain with his sword held out in front of him.

Hector stepped out from behind the chariot to face his opponent. Achilles, edging closer, saw the big man grip his spear

tightly, preparing to throw. He saw his powerful muscles and his determined stance.

But for a split second, through the slits in Hector's stolen helmet, Achilles also caught a glimpse of his enemy's cold, staring eyes.

And in them, he saw something that gave him hope.

He saw fear.

"PREPARE TO *DIE!*" Achilles bellowed, rushing at Hector in a

furious rage. The Trojan drew back his spear and tried to aim, but before he was ready to throw, his courage deserted him. He dropped the spear clumsily, and took the only course of action left open to him.

He ran.

Up on the walls of Troy, Queen Hecuba and King Priam watched in horror, clutching each other's hands tightly.

"Don't look," whispered Priam in a broken voice, and his wife buried her face in his shoulder he as gathered her, sobbing, into his arms.

"*Yes!*" Achilles muttered between clenched teeth, his determination fired up even more by the cowardice of the man who had killed his best friend. "Now I'm going to get you once and for all!" Hector's stumbling, terrified figure was only paces away from him now.

"REVENGE!" roared Achilles, as he closed in on his prey.

At that moment, the gods were engaged in a loud discussion about what exactly should be done.

"The Trojans have had their fair share of success," boomed Hera. "It's time for the Greeks to win for a change."

"I agree," said Athene, nodding wisely.

"Well, if I'm not mistaken, you've already been helping your darling Achilles," said Apollo. "And don't pretend it was the wind that blew Hector's spear away."

"I'm not pretending," sniffed Athene. "And you're a fine one to talk! I think we all know where that strange mist came from, hiding your precious Hector just in time. And didn't he have a tiny little bit of help in killing poor Patroclus?"

Apollo scowled.

"All this bickering is getting us nowhere," sighed Zeus. "The point is, what are we going to do? Is Hector going to escape this time, or is Achilles going to kill him?"

At the thought of Hector being killed, Aphrodite burst into tears. Everyone else groaned. There was a stony silence. Then Zeus took a deep breath and spoke.

"I don't think we're going to come to an agreement on this. So. . there's only one thing to do. I'll have to get out my scales."

The others exchanged surprised glances. Zeus only ever used his scales as a last resort. Things must be serious.

Zeus stood up and rummaged on a shelf behind his throne.

"I know they're here somewhere," he muttered.

"What's that at the back?" said

Apollo, peering with difficulty past his father's shaggy hair.

"Aha!" said Zeus triumphantly. He lifted down a pair of golden weighing scales. After blowing the dust off them, he reached inside his robe and pulled out a small leather bag marked 'Death Powder'. Opening it carefully, he measured out two portions of the shiny black grains, one into each scale.

"The one on my left is Achilles's death portion," he explained when he'd finished. "And the one on my right is Hector's. Now, let's see. . . "

Meanwhile, Andromache was in the palace, boiling a cauldron of hot water for Hector's evening bath. She liked to have it ready for him when he staggered in exhausted from battle. Humming softly as she plucked a clean linen towel from the chest, she wondered whether today had been as successful as Hector had hoped it would be.

The baby gurgled noisily in his high chair, banging his tiny fists on its wooden sides.

"Hello little sparrow!" Andromache cooed. "Are you missing your father? I expect he'll be home soon – don't you fret."

At that moment, a servant girl appeared

in the doorway.

"Madam, there's a messenger here to see you," she said.

"Oh, all right. Send him in," Andromache sighed, adding under her breath, "He's probably come to tell me that the battle's going to go on all night."

The messenger stepped into the room, cleared his throat and said loudly, "Madam, King Priam has sent me. You're to come to the city wall immediately."

"Why, whatever's happened?" asked Andromache.

The messenger shuffled his feet and looked uncomfortable.

"I don't know, Madam. He just said you should come at once."

Something about his tone of voice frightened Andromache. She snatched up her cloak and, calling to her maidservant to look after the baby, hurried out of the palace.

When she arrived at the wall, quite a crowd was gathered there. Priam saw her approaching and stepped forward to meet her. The minute she saw his face, she knew something was terribly wrong.

"What is it?" she cried, grabbing hold of his outstretched hands. "Is it Hector? Is he wounded? *Tell* me!"

Priam's face crumpled and he clung to her arm like a child. He opened his mouth to speak but all that came out was a strangled moan.

Andromache shook him off and pushed her way through the crowd. Hecuba was crouching down, her back against the wall, with Paris bending over her. Her face was covered by her hands but she was wailing loudly as if in great pain.

Stepping past her, the fear rising in her throat, Andromache looked over the wall, down to the plain below. For a moment, all she could see were hordes of Greek soldiers some distance away. She scanned the battlefield.

Then she saw Hector. He was lying still on the dusty ground.

Andromache's head started to spin, and she felt dizzy. She clutched at the top of the wall to steady herself.

"No!" she murmured, closing her eyes. "Please don't let it be true."

But when she looked again, he was still there.

Andromache's legs gave way beneath her and she clung to the wall. Suddenly she remembered that she'd left the cauldron over the fire.

"The water will boil dry," she mumbled, then realized it no longer mattered.

Hector wouldn't be coming home for his bath.

She felt Paris's hand on her shoulder.

"He was so brave," he lied,

blocking out of his mind the awful image of his brother, running desperately from the terrible might of Achilles, hounded shamefully to death, like a fox or a rat.

"He fought back right up to the last minute," Paris went on. "You should be proud of him."

Andromache couldn't speak. She couldn't cry. She could hear Hecuba sobbing nearby, but she couldn't make a sound.

Priam stumbled up behind her and took her arm. Then the three of them, wife, brother and father-in-law, stood staring down in silence at the body, while Hecuba, Hector's devoted mother, lay crumpled on the ground next to them, weeping hopelessly.

As they watched, a Greek soldier walked coldly up to the body and crouched on the ground next to it. Andromache had never seen him before,

but she knew well who it must be. Achilles.

When Achilles stood up, they saw that he had tied long leather straps around Hector's ankles.

"What's he doing?" gasped Paris in outrage.

Achilles then picked up the loose ends of the straps and walked the few steps to his chariot. He tied the straps to the back of it, climbed in and took hold of the reins.

"No!" groaned Priam, his voice choking with grief.

The horses jumped to a start. Andromache brought her hands up to her face in utter horror. Then, the tears began to squeeze from her eyes as she watched the chariot go charging over the plain, with the body of her beloved husband bumping along behind it in the dust.

Chapter eight

BURYING THE DEAD

Achilles was miserable. It was the day after he'd killed Hector, but instead of feeling triumphant, he felt utterly depressed.

He'd just returned from his best friend's funeral. Patroclus had been given all the attention a true hero deserved. The servants had made an enormous pile of all the branches and twigs they could find, and laid the body on top before setting light to the wood.

Achilles had watched, grief-stricken, as the flames licked higher and higher. The fire burned all day long, and the Greek soldiers came in groups to pay their last respects. In the evening, all that was left of Patroclus's body was a small heap of charred bones, which were gathered up, wrapped in soft material and placed in a beautiful gold urn.

Now Achilles was left with a sense of emptiness. He'd killed Hector, but where did that get him? He was one of the greatest fighters in the world, but even he was powerless to bring back Patroclus, his dear friend and comrade. He was starting to wonder what the point of all this fighting was – so many meaningless deaths, and all for the sake of a woman. Would they ever get Helen back?

The urn containing Patroclus's bones now stood in a corner of Achilles's tent. As he stared at it, his mind wandering, he heard someone behind him. Turning around, he saw his servant girl, Briseis. Agamemnon had returned her when Achilles had rejoined the war.

"He was a wonderful man," Briseis said, gazing sadly at the golden urn. "He was always very kind to me – almost as if I were his sister."

"I feel so guilty," sighed Achilles. "*Why* did I let him go into battle? If only I'd said no, he'd still be here now, pouring the wine and cutting up the meat. . . "

"He wanted to fight," Briseis reminded him. "It was his choice. At least they managed to retrieve his body from the field. Think how much worse you'd feel if you hadn't

"When I die, I want *my* bones to be put in the same urn. Then we can be buried together."

Wiping away a few tears, Briseis left him to his grief and began to prepare a meal.

For days, Achilles remained distraught. He continued to fight on the battlefield, but each time he came back to his tent and saw the golden urn in the corner, he felt that everything was pointless.

Each evening, he took out his frustration in a terrible way. Hector's body still lay on the dirty ground behind the tent, the leather straps still tied around his ankles.

even been able to give him a proper funeral."

Achilles just shrugged.

"Perhaps you should try and get some rest," suggested Briseis. "Did you sleep at all last night?"

Achilles shook his head. He'd spent the night out on the beach, sitting on the damp sand and watching the rhythmic movement of the dark waves beating on the shore.

After a long silence, he said, "I'm going to keep his bones."

"Aren't you going to bury them?" asked Briseis in surprise.

Achilles yoked his horses to his chariot, fastened the straps to the back of it and climbed in. Then he drove up and down the shore, dragging the body behind him. When he was exhausted, he untied the straps and left Hector sprawling with his face in the dirt.

From Zeus's palace, the gods were keeping an eye on Achilles. The longer he went on behaving in this way, the more concerned they became. Finally, after almost two weeks, Aphrodite could bear it no longer and called an urgent meeting.

"We *have* to do something," she

insisted, when everyone was seated and the cups of nectar had been handed around. "We can't just stand by and watch him treating Hector's body so shamefully – it's not right."

"Hear, hear!" chimed in Apollo. "Something must be done."

Zeus glanced over at his wife.

"Well, Hera?" he asked. "What do you think?"

Hera paused for a moment. Then she said, "I agree."

There was a stunned silence. Hera hardly ever agreed with anyone.

"I'm pleased that Achilles killed Hector," she continued, "and I still want the Greeks to win the war. . . but I agree that his treatment of the body is wrong and should be stopped."

"Well!" exclaimed Apollo, raising his eyebrows. "I never thought I'd hear *you* sympathize with a Trojan!"

Hera scowled at him.

"Athene?" said Zeus. "What about you?"

"I agree with Hera," said Athene, ignoring Apollo's triumphant smile. "I think Hector's body should be returned to his parents so they can bury him properly. No one deserves to be treated like that – not even a Trojan."

"So we're all agreed," said Zeus, sounding very relieved – and rather surprised.

"The question is – what are we going to do about it?" asked Apollo.

"Couldn't we just steal Hector's body and give it back to his family?" suggested Athene.

"No," said Zeus firmly. "I want Achilles to give up the body of his own accord."

"Well perhaps we could send Thetis to talk to him," said Aphrodite. "She's terribly worried about him – he hasn't slept or eaten for days."

"Good idea!" said Apollo.

They all looked expectantly at Zeus to make the final decision. But he just said, "Would somebody please summon Hermes – I have an urgent message for him to deliver."

Meanwhile, in Troy, the whole city was in mourning. Priam and Hecuba mostly stayed closeted away in their rooms, overcome by grief. Their daughter, Cassandra, did her best to comfort them.

But Paris tried to avoid his parents. He couldn't help feeling that they blamed him for Hector's death – and probably for Polydorus's too.

Helen wandered the corridors, weeping for Hector, who'd always

been kind to her. As for Andromache, she never left her chamber. She refused to see anyone but her servant girls and her baby son.

One evening, Priam was sitting alone leaning against a pillar in the courtyard with his head in his hands. Suddenly Hermes appeared in front of him. Priam jumped to his feet.

"King Priam," Hermes announced. "Zeus has sent me. Load a wagon with treasure, find a driver and hitch up some mules – you must go to Achilles to ask for Hector's body."

The old man had struggled to his feet as soon as he saw the messenger god. He recognized him instantly by the wings on his sandals.

"But he'll kill me!" he gasped.

"No he won't," replied Hermes. "I promise I'll take care of you. Now do as I say."

And he disappeared.

So Priam ordered his men to get the wagon ready, and hurried off to the storeroom with two servants. He found Hecuba there, rummaging through a chest of Hector's clothes, her eyes red from crying. When he told her about Hermes's message, she burst into tears again.

"What?" she sobbed. "Go to Achilles's tent all by yourself? To the Greek camp? At night? But they'll kill you! *No*, Priam! I've lost two sons – I can't bear to lose my husband too."

"It's an order from Zeus," said

Suddenly Hermes appeared in front of him

Priam gently, as he went over to a chest and lifted the lid. He picked out twelve fine fur cloaks, twelve beautifully embroidered cotton tunics and twelve soft wool blankets, and loaded the servants' arms with the gifts. From another chest, he carefully lifted two gold lamp stands and a silver goblet covered with intricate engravings.

"You're *not* going, Priam," said Hecuba, her voice trembling. "I won't allow it."

"I *have* to go. It's our only chance to get Hector's body back. Do you want him to lie unburied in an enemy camp? Don't you think he deserves a proper funeral?"

A short while later, the treasure had been loaded onto the back of the wagon. Night had now fallen and the courtyard was in darkness. Idaius the driver climbed onto the wagon seat and shouted at the mules. Hecuba watched in silence.

"Goodbye, Hecuba," said Priam, as he stepped into his chariot and picked up the reins. "Pray that I'll return safely – with Hector."

And he drove out of the courtyard, along the city streets and through the gate onto the open plain, with the wagon rattling along behind.

Priam felt very nervous outside the city. He peered into the distance, scanning the field for enemies, but there was no one in sight. When they had been rolling across the plain for some time, the shadowy shape of the Greek wall loomed out of the darkness ahead, eerily lit by the full moon.

Idaius stopped his horses and called quietly to Priam.

"How will we get through? There's bound to be sentries on guard – I think I can see their fires."

As if in answer to his question, Hermes appeared.

"Follow me," he ordered. He led them close to the wall, then leaped into the air and soared up to the top. Balancing for a moment on the battlements, he quickly put all the sentries to sleep before flying down to open one of the gates.

"But the ditch – we'll never manage to cross it," whispered Idaius.

Almost as he spoke, a bridge of wooden planks appeared, leading across the ditch to the open gate. Hermes beckoned silently and the two vehicles trundled safely over the bridge and through the gateway. Priam glanced back and saw the sentries fast asleep beside their fires, their heads lolling back and their mouths wide open.

With Hermes flying ahead, they made their way through the enemy camp. Priam felt sick and his palms were sweating so much, he could hardly keep hold of the reins. He was terrified that someone would hear them and raise the alarm. But they drove unnoticed past the rows of tents and ships, until at last they came to the far end.

"This is Achilles's tent," said Hermes, landing gracefully and pointing to the left. "I'm going to leave you now, but I'll be back later."

Priam looked uncertain.

"What am I to do?" he asked.

"Go in and talk to him," replied Hermes. "Ask him for your son's body."

"But what if. . . ?" began Priam. But Hermes had vanished.

Priam waited a while, hoping the god might return, then climbed shakily down from his chariot.

"Wait for me here," he said to Idaius, who nodded silently.

Priam's breath was shallow and he was quaking inside, but he took a deep breath and strode to the tent.

Inside, Achilles's companions had just finished eating. The table was strewn with the remains of their meal. Achilles himself was sitting on a chair with his back to the others, a plate of half-eaten food on his lap. He was staring absent-mindedly into the middle distance when, to his astonishment, an old man suddenly appeared in the doorway. As Achilles leaped to his feet, the plate crashed

to the ground and everyone looked up, startled.

Priam stood just inside the tent. He was too scared to say anything.

No one knew who he was, but they could tell by his appearance that he wasn't a Greek. Some of the men started reaching for their weapons, but Achilles motioned to them to keep still. After observing the stranger's face for several seconds, he sat down again.

"Well, old man," he said. "You gave us all a shock. We're not used to strangers arriving in the middle of the night without warning. Where have you come from?"

A note of gentleness in Achilles's voice gave Priam the courage to speak.

He stepped forward and fell onto his knees in front of Achilles's chair. Kneeling humbly at the young man's feet, he said simply, "Sir, my name is Priam, King of Troy."

A gasp of amazement rippled around the tent.

"I've come here to beg you to give me back my son's body," continued Priam. "My wife was afraid you would kill me, but I hoped you'd have pity. I couldn't live the rest of my life knowing Hector had not been buried. . . "

His voice began to quiver, and he glanced up at Achilles, unsure whether or not to go on.

"There's a wagon full of gifts for you outside – I'll bring more if you want. . . " he added tentatively.

Achilles looked down at the old man's blood-shot eyes and wrinkled face. He

was reminded of his own father, Peleus, far away in Greece. Achilles had gone to say goodbye to him before leaving for Troy, but that was years ago now. He realized with a shock that his father might not even be alive when the war ended.

"You're a brave man, King Priam, to come here alone," he said at last. "Your son would be proud of you."

Priam bowed his head.

"Why don't you rest for a while?" continued Achilles. "You look exhausted. I'll have my men prepare some food for you."

"Sir," mumbled Priam. "You are very kind – but all I want from you is my son's body."

"You will have your son's body in due course, but there's something I must do first. Have some food while you're waiting."

"I couldn't eat anything, sir," replied the old man, "but I would be glad to rest – I have hardly slept since. . . ."

Achilles just nodded.

"Lie down on the couch and try to sleep. I'll wake you as soon as we're ready."

"There's one more thing," said Priam as he sank down onto the couch. "We need to gather wood for the funeral, but my people are afraid to come out of the city in case they are attacked."

"How long do you need to mourn your son and prepare for the funeral?" asked Achilles.

"Ten days should be enough," said Priam hopefully.

"Well, I will make sure the fighting is stopped for that time. Now lie down and sleep."

Priam took some sips of water from a cup brought to him by Briseis. Then he slipped off his sandals, lay down and fell asleep within minutes.

When the king awoke, it was dawn, and for a moment he wasn't sure where he was. Someone had spread a blanket over him while he slept. Pushing it aside, he got to his feet and stepped quietly outside.

His chariot stood where he had left it, the horses tethered to a nearby post. Idaius was lying in the wagon seat, snoring loudly. And in the back of the wagon, in place of the gifts he had brought, Priam saw the body, carefully cleaned and wrapped in a beautiful cloak. Although Hector's face was horribly disfigured, the old man had no trouble recognizing his beloved son.

He reached out a hand and laid it gently on Hector's head. As he stood there weeping silently, Hermes appeared again.

"It's time to leave," he said.

Priam nodded and wiped the tears from his eyes. He shook Idaius awake and climbed into his chariot. Then they set off back to the city.

The battle was raging again near the city wall. With Hector dead and Achilles back in action, the Trojans were by far the weaker side. Paris had tried to take over from his brother, but he knew he could never command the same respect.

Since Hector's funeral, he'd been feeling guilty. He cast his mind back to his days as a shepherd and almost wished he'd never returned to Troy. If only he could do something to make his parents proud of him, like they had been of Hector. The trouble was, he knew he wasn't brave enough.

Whenever the fighting grew fierce, Paris would keep as close as possible to the gate, so that he could escape into the city if necessary. He was there now, lurking by the gatepost, his bow in his hand. Swords and spears were clashing all around and the dust was flying everywhere. Suddenly, he spotted Achilles nearby.

He lifted up his bow. With trembling fingers, he positioned an arrow and drew back the taut string. But he couldn't bring himself to let go. Every time he was about to fire, his nerve failed him. He couldn't help thinking about what Achilles might do to him if he survived the blow. He'd kill him, just as humiliatingly as he'd killed poor Hector. And the truth was, Paris was terrified of dying.

Just as he was about to give up and sneak back into the city for a rest, he heard a strange voice whispering in his ear.

"Go on Paris! You can do it! Just take aim and fire. Think how proud your father will be. You'll be the avenger of your brother's death. The whole city will salute you as a hero. Go on! Fire!"

Paris was startled. He glanced behind him but there was no one there. Spurred on by the peculiar voice, he could feel his heart beating faster. Achilles was still in his line of vision. Leaning back against the gatepost to steady himself, Paris raised his bow again, took aim – and fired.

The arrow zoomed away. Paris had aimed too low and, for a moment, it looked as if the weapon would land in the dust, harming no one. But Apollo was watching. He took a deep breath and blew as hard as he could under the arrow, so that it skimmed along just above the ground.

Achilles was busy engaging in a violent swordfight with a Trojan soldier. He cursed as he felt a sudden thudding pain in his left heel. Someone's badly aimed arrow must have lodged there. Now he'd have to leave the battlefield to have his foot bandaged, just as he was getting into his stride.

But when Achilles tried to reach for the arrow to pull it out, he stumbled and fell. Something was wrong. Why was it that the searing pain from his heel seemed to spread through him, crippling his limbs and clutching at his heart?

"Help me!" shouted Achilles, the blood draining from his face.

Ulysses was fighting nearby. He ran to Achilles's side and tried to pull the arrow out of the wound. Achilles screamed with pain. Greek soldiers began to gather around to see what was going on.

"Get back to the battle!" ordered Ulysses. "I'll take care of him."

But the battle had come to a standstill, as both sides looked on in amazement. Someone had felled the mighty Achilles!

Paris was still cowering by the gate, hardly able to believe his eyes. He saw Achilles lying curled up on the ground, the arrow still protruding from his foot at an awkward angle. For a while, his whole body seemed racked with tension. Then, after a sudden jerking movement, he lay still.

Thetis was in her father's cave at the bottom of the sea. She was sitting on a giant shell, making garlands of seaweed and gossiping with her sisters. All of a sudden, an icy chill ran through her body.

"What is it?" Nereus asked his daughter, noticing she'd turned very pale.

"It's Achilles. . ." wailed Thetis. "I – I think he's dead!"

The other sea nymphs stared at her in horror.

"Dead!" exclaimed Nereus. "Surely not. How do you know?"

"I just *know*," sobbed Thetis. "But I don't understand. He *can't* be dead – I made him immortal. He's supposed to live forever. . . I must go to him immediately."

She rushed out of the cave, glided up to the surface of the sea and burst out of the water into the air. She flew as fast as she could until she came to Troy. Circling over a wide area, she desperately scanned the plain below for a glimpse of her beloved son.

Then she spotted a small group of men marching away from the fighting. Flying lower, she saw that they were carrying someone on a stretcher. And she knew immediately that it was Achilles.

She swooped closer until she could see his face – it was frighteningly white and lifeless, and she knew then that he really was dead. Tears trickled down her cheeks and she wiped them away as she quickly scanned his body for any sign of injury. As soon as she saw the gaping wound in the back of his foot, where Paris's arrow had penetrated, her mind flew back to that day when she'd dipped the baby Achilles into the River Styx – *holding him by his tiny heel.*

"His heel!" she gasped, realizing with a dreadful shock what had happened. "His heel's still mortal – it never touched the water!"

And the prediction Chiron the centaur had made all those years ago began ringing in her ears. . . "*The Greek army will never capture Troy unless Achilles fights with them, and Achilles will die fighting there.*"

That evening, Agamemnon sat in his tent, his head in his hands.

"Achilles," he groaned. "Our best fighter, such a fine young man. Just when we were winning. . . Oh Menelaus, whatever next?" he sighed, staring wearily at his brother.

"It's as if we're cursed," said Menelaus grimly. He felt terrible. He still longed to get Helen back, but so many men were dying – so many great men, lost forever because of what he, Menelaus, wanted.

Just then, a herald appeared in the doorway.

"There's a servant girl here to see you, sir," he announced.

Agamemnon looked up, surprised.

"All right," he said resignedly. "Show her in."

Briseis, Achilles's servant girl, slipped nervously into the tent. She had clearly been crying. Agamemnon looked at her kindly.

"What can I do for you, Briseis?" he asked.

"I wanted to tell you something, sir," she answered.

"Go on," said the king.

"It's something Achilles said to me a while ago."

They waited for her to continue.

"He was keeping Patroclus's bones in a golden urn in his tent. He said that when he died, he wanted *his* bones to be put into the same urn, so they could be buried together." She looked at Agamemnon.

He nodded.

"Then that's what we'll do," he said. "After Achilles's funeral, we'll bury them together in a grave by the sea."

"Oh thank you, sir," said Briseis, running forward and kissing his hand. Then she turned and hurried out through the doorway.

Ulysses, who was sitting on the other side of the tent, watched the two brothers sadly, wishing there was some way he could turn their fortunes around. Without Achilles, there was no way they could fight their way out of this.

He must be able to come up with a plan. If he really put his mind to it. . .

Chapter nine

THE WOODEN HORSE

Early one morning, not long after Paris had killed Achilles, Priam was wandering through the streets of Troy. Since Hector's death, he'd had trouble sleeping, and had taken to going for long walks by himself.

Hecuba was still so upset, he could hardly bear to spend time with her. And grief wasn't the only thing on his mind – he was rapidly losing any hope that the war was ever going to end. Now that both sides had lost their best warriors, there was a lack of direction in the fighting.

After roaming around for some time, he found himself near the wall. He climbed to the top and came upon a group of guards huddled together, deep in conversation. As soon as they spotted him, they called him over.

"Sir, come and see!"

Priam hurried to join them and looked out over the wall. He could hardly believe what he saw.

Some distance from the city, in the middle of the plain, stood a huge wooden horse.

"Whatever is it?" said Priam in bewilderment.

"Looks like a horse, sir," said one of the guards.

Priam glared at him.

"I can see that," he said impatiently. "But what on earth is it doing there?"

"No one knows, sir," replied the guard. "It was there at first light, so it must have arrived in the night. And that's not all, sir. The Greeks have gone. Vanished. Completely disappeared."

Priam stared at him in disbelief.

"It's true, sir," said another guard. "A group of men have been down to the shore. The camp's been dismantled and the ships that were left have gone. Looks like the Greeks have given up and sailed home."

Priam was stunned. But before he could collect his thoughts, he heard the sound of voices at the gate below. A minute later, two guards appeared at the top of the steps. Between them, struggling hard, was a young man. His clothes were torn and filthy, and he looked terrified.

"We found him hiding near the shore, sir," explained one of the guards. "He claims to be a deserter from the Greek army." As he spoke, he twisted the man's arm roughly behind his back, causing him to cry out in pain.

"Let go of him," ordered Priam. The guards reluctantly obeyed.

"Tell me who you are," he said.

"My name is Sinon, sir," replied the trembling prisoner.

"And you are with the Greek army?"

"Well, I was," replied the man, rubbing his aching arm. "But when I heard they were planning to leave in the night and sail back to Greece, I ran away and hid until they'd gone. I couldn't face the long journey back – there's nothing for me to go home for anyway. Besides, I'm sick of being ordered around all the time. . . " He paused to draw breath and looked nervously up at Priam.

"Why have the Greeks left?" asked Priam.

"King Agamemnon decided they were never going to break into the city, especially now that Achilles is dead. And Menelaus agreed that enough men had lost their lives and it was time to call a halt to the whole thing. So they packed up and left."

"And the horse?"

"It's supposed to be a gift to Athene," said Sinon. "Calchas the soothsayer told Agamemnon it would help to ensure a safe journey home. He also said. . . "

"Go on," said the king.

". . . that if the horse was brought inside the city gates, Athene would protect Troy and it would never be taken by enemies."

The guards exchanged suspicious glances and Priam didn't know whether to believe the man or not. He decided to go home and think things over.

By the time he got back to the palace, news of the wooden horse and of the Greeks' departure had already begun to spread around the city. Hecuba and Cassandra were waiting eagerly for his return. When he told them what Sinon had said, Hecuba smiled for the first time in weeks.

"Maybe it's a sign that things are going to get better," she said. "What are you going to do, Priam?"

"Well, I don't see what harm it would do to bring the horse into the city," replied Priam. "And if the man's speaking the truth, it could do us a lot of good."

"*If* he's speaking the truth," interrupted Cassandra. "It's a trap, Father – I'm certain of it. Why should we believe what a Greek says?"

"He had an honest face," said Priam.

Cassandra groaned and threw her hands up in despair.

"Father, you're so trusting. Just because someone 'has an honest face', you're prepared to risk everything."

"But what's the risk?" asked her father.

"Oh never mind!" snapped Cassandra and she flounced out of the room.

Later that day, the gates were opened. Hordes of old people, servants, women and children swarmed out onto the plain, singing and shouting with joy. They'd been trapped inside the city for so long, they hardly remembered what it was like to go outside. They crowded around the strange horse, jumping up to rap on its body, stroking its smooth wooden legs and gasping at its incredible size. Mothers lifted up their children who laughed in delight at its long, tapering nose and sharply pointed ears.

Long ropes were brought from the city and attached to the horse. Then fifty of the strongest men took hold of the ends and began to pull. Although the horse had been built on large, wooden wheels, it was hard work moving it across the plain's rough surface. It also seemed surprisingly heavy.

Puffing and panting, the men slowly dragged the horse closer and closer to the city, cheered on by hundreds of watching citizens. Through the gateway they guided the enormous object, being careful not to scrape its sides. They pulled it along the streets, all the way to the marketplace.

And there it stood for the rest of the day – the most amazing sight anyone in Troy had ever seen.

That evening, the Trojans feasted until late into the night. For the first time in years, the city gates and walls could be left unguarded and everyone could enjoy themselves without fear of a sudden attack. The Greeks had gone, and the war was over at last!

Finally, in the early hours of the morning, they sank into their beds, exhausted but exhilarated, and slept soundly.

Inside the horse's hollow body, it was stiflingly hot. Menelaus wiped the sweat from his forehead and sighed loudly.

"Shhhh!" hissed Ulysses.

"It's been quiet outside for ages now," whispered Menelaus. "Surely it's safe to take a look?"

The others murmured in agreement. There were twelve of them, and they'd been inside the horse since the previous night. The tension was unbearable. For many hours now, they'd been sitting absolutely still, hardly daring to move a muscle, clutching their weapons close to their bodies, for fear a slight rattle of metal against wood might give them away.

Diomedes had his ear pressed against the side of the horse.

"There's no sign of life out there," he said. "They *must* have gone to bed by now."

Ulysses thought for a while. Building the horse had been his idea, so he felt responsible for the outcome. Things had gone smoothly so far and he didn't want to waste all their hard work by being impatient at the last minute. Still, it *was* very quiet outside. And they couldn't afford to wait too long. Once morning came, it would be too late. Ulysses finally decided it was time to act.

"All right," he said, quietly but firmly. "I'm going to run through the plan one more time. Is everyone listening?"

The others nodded.

"First," Ulysses whispered, "we climb out of the horse, try to get our

And there it stood for the rest of the day. . .

. . .the most amazing sight anyone in Troy had ever seen

bearings, then make our way to the gates – all in absolute silence. When we find the gates, we'll have to unlock them— "

"What if they're guarded?" interrupted Diomedes.

"We'll just have to hope they won't be," said Ulysses. "If Sinon was convincing enough, the Trojans should think we've gone for good. Then, hopefully, the rest of the army will have sailed back during the night and will be waiting outside the city."

"If Sinon managed to signal to them," said Menelaus.

"How will we know if he did?" asked Diomedes.

"We *won't!*" snapped Menelaus impatiently.

"Be quiet!" hissed Ulysses. "Then, assuming the army *is* waiting outside the gates, we let them in – and destroy the city."

It sounded straightforward, but the men knew what a dangerous situation they were in. Some clenched their fists, and others breathed deeply as they prepared themselves for the attack. It was their last chance.

"Diomedes," said Ulysses. "Open the trapdoor. And everyone else – keep still and don't make a sound."

⬩⬤⬤⬤⬤⬤⬤⬤⬤⬤⬤⬩

Paris awoke suddenly. He lay still for a few minutes, wondering what had disturbed him. Somewhere in the distance, he could hear voices shouting. At first, he thought it was just the celebrations still going on. But as the sounds grew louder, he wasn't so sure. Deciding to go and investigate, he slipped out of bed, dressed quickly and walked through the silent corridors.

As soon as he opened the palace gate, he realized that something was wrong. Over to his right, spirals of smoke were swirling up into the sky above the city. And the voices he'd heard before were coming closer all the time. They weren't the happy sounds of merrymakers wending their way home from a feast. They were the screams and shouts of terrified people.

"What's going on?" muttered Paris under his breath.

Then he spotted a group of bedraggled citizens fleeing around the corner. As they came closer, Paris stepped out into the street.

"What is it?" he shouted. "What's happening? Is your house on fire?"

The oldest member of the group slowed down enough to reply.

"More like the whole city, sir! The Greeks have come back – they're destroying everything and killing everyone. . . and they're heading this way!"

One of his companions tugged at his sleeve and they hurried on their way. Behind them came more people – small groups at first, then larger ones, until there was a constant stream of citizens fleeing past the palace. Old men and women stumbling along with sticks, families with screaming babies and wailing toddlers, younger, fitter people overtaking the slower ones, all of them frantic with fear.

As Paris watched, his mind started racing.

This could be his chance. If he acted now, he might be able to save the city. He decided to go back to the palace for his weapons. Then he'd go and fight off those Greeks once and for all. He knew there wouldn't be many of them – probably just a small contingent that had returned to cause trouble.

Minutes later, he was back at the gate, fully armed. He strode through the city, heading in the opposite direction from everyone else. By now, the streets were so packed with people, he had to fight his way through. As he approached the marketplace, the smell of burning wood filled his nostrils and the noise was deafening. Blood-curdling screams rang out from every building, and flames sprang from windows and doorways.

In the panic, nobody recognized Paris. They jostled past him, desperate to get as far from the danger as possible.

"Don't go that way!" shouted a young woman as she struggled by, a small child clinging to each arm. "The Greeks will kill you!"

Paris pushed on until, at last, he stepped into the marketplace. There stood the huge wooden horse, a trapdoor swinging open from its belly. All around, Paris gazed upon a scene he could never have imagined in his wildest dreams.

Instead of the small group of Greeks he had expected, he saw what looked like the whole army surging in his direction. In that enclosed and familiar space, the soldiers appeared much larger and far more formidable than they ever had out on the plain. Brandishing their mighty weapons and yelling war cries, they were killing everyone they could see, and destroying whatever stood in their path.

Paris immediately had second thoughts about being a hero. He turned to join the escaping hordes – just as an arrow came whistling through the air, heading straight for his back.

"Look out!" screamed an old woman.

But her warning came too late.

Before Paris knew what was happening, the arrow hit his shoulder and pierced right through to his heart. He clutched at his chest, moaning with agony, as blood began to spurt from the wound. Staggering forward a few steps, he grabbed hold of a marble pillar and leaned heavily against it. The pain was unbearable. Slowly, his hands slipped down the pillar, smearing its smooth white surface with streaks of blood. Then he slumped to the ground in a heap.

Priam was woken by a piercing scream. He rose from his bed and stumbled to the door. Hecuba and Cassandra were in the corridor, weeping and shivering in their nightgowns, with a small group of servants cowering nearby.

"What is it?" asked Priam. "Who screamed?"

One of the servants spoke up.

"The Greeks have come back, sir," he spluttered. "They're destroying the city. . . setting fire to everything, killing all the men and capturing all the women and children—"

"They've killed Paris!" sobbed Hecuba. "He went out to try and fight them off and they've killed him!"

Priam stared at them, dazed with horror. His dear children, Polydorus, Hector, and now Paris too – all gone, sacrificed to this terrible, pointless war.

He remembered, all those years ago, hearing the prediction that his baby son, Paris, would bring about the destruction of Troy. He thought, too late, of Cassandra's unheeded warnings. The king felt bewildered, trapped in a nightmare that never seemed to end. . . and he sank to his knees as the sound of clashing swords, heavy footsteps and shouts began to echo through the palace.

A maidservant came tearing along the corridor.

"The soldiers are here!" she screamed. "They've broken through the palace gates – and they're coming this— "

Before she could finish, a group of soldiers, led by Ulysses, burst through the door at the end of the corridor and marched over to where the family stood.

Priam stepped forward.

"I am King Priam," he said, his voice quivering, "and this is my home. I will hand over anything you ask for, but I beg you not to harm my family or my servants."

Ulysses stared at the old man for a few seconds, then looked away.

"Search the palace!" he ordered. "Kill the men and take the women as prisoners – but don't hurt them."

The soldiers split up into smaller groups and set off in different directions. One of them approached Hecuba and grabbed her by the arm. She struggled to break free, but he held her firmly until he had tied her hands together behind her back. Twisting around, she saw another soldier doing the same to Cassandra. He tied the rope tightly, and the girl cried out in pain.

"Loosen it!" commanded Ulysses immediately.

As Priam watched helplessly, more footsteps approached. Two of the soldiers reappeared, bringing Helen and Andromache with them. Helen was weeping uncontrollably.

As she passed Priam, she looked up at him palely and opened her mouth to speak. But she could say nothing. Her head was spinning. All she knew was that she'd never meant it to end like this – so much destruction, so many horrific deaths.

If only Paris could protect her. Or Menelaus. . .

Andromache glided past as if she were in a dream, her hands tied behind her back and her head bowed. She didn't seem to notice anyone or anything.

The soldiers began to lead all the women away. Hecuba turned her head to look at Priam. He was heartbroken, his blank face staring confusedly ahead. He glanced at her with faint recognition.

"Please don't hurt my husband!" she called over her shoulder. "He's an old man. . . "

But as she turned the corner, and Priam disappeared from view, she knew she would never see him again.

Feeling guilty and ashamed, Ulysses stared down at the ground. So this was how the war was to end. Women being dragged away from their homes, old men spending their last few moments in terror, families being torn apart. . .

He remembered how excited he'd felt when they'd arrived at Troy and had set up camp on the shore. How could he have imagined then that he'd still be here all these years later! He thought of the family he'd left behind in Ithaca – his wife Penelope and their young son. He'd

been away for so long, he wondered if he'd even recognize the boy. Still, with any luck, he'd soon be home.

Shaking himself out of his reverie, he tightened his grip on his spear and marched off to make a final search of the palace.

The gods were sitting in a grassy meadow on the slopes of Mount Olympus, relaxing in the sunshine and discussing the end of the war.

"I knew the Greeks would win in the end!" said Athene proudly.

"So did I," said Hera.

Apollo snorted grumpily and turned his back on them.

"I don't think it's anything to be proud of," said Zeus sternly. "War is such an unpleasant business. But those humans *will* keep killing each other," he sighed. "I'm just relieved it's all over.

"And," he added, turning to his wife, "I'm sorry. I – well, I haven't been quite myself recently." He didn't want to mention Thetis.

Hera said nothing. She just took his hand and smiled forgivingly.

Aphrodite wandered up, a slight scowl on her face. She'd been sulking ever since the war ended.

"Come on, my dear!" Zeus chided her gently. "Let's put this behind us, shall we?"

Aphrodite looked up at him defiantly. Zeus tried again.

"It's all over now," he said, "and thank goodness everything's back to normal. The Greeks have Helen back, and that's all there is to it!"

"Oh, look!" exclaimed Aphrodite all of a sudden, her frown disappearing completely. "Look down there!"

"What?" demanded Athene. They all got up and peered down at the Trojan shore, where the Greeks were packing up and preparing to leave.

"He's taking her back!" cried Aphrodite happily. "Look – he still loves her! Oh, how sweet!"

Menelaus and Helen were standing together on the beach. As the first few Greek ships began to sail away from Troy, their huge white sails billowing in the wind, Helen tossed her still beautiful curls and smiled up at her husband.

Menelaus, wiping away tears of joy from his face, bent down and kissed her tenderly.

Then he took her gently by the arm, and, with one last glance over his shoulder at the broad Trojan plain, he led his wife across the gangplank, and onto his ship.

WHO'S WHO

Achilles (a-*kill*-ees) Son of Peleus and Thetis. One of the Greek leaders and their best soldier. Withdraws from the fighting after an argument with Agamemnon, but returns after his friend, Patroclus, is killed while pretending to be him. Kills Hector, and is killed by Paris.

Agamemnon (ag-a-*mem*-non) King of Mycenae and brother of Menelaus. Commander of the Greek armies.

Ajax (*age*-ax) Greek soldier. Very strong.

Andromache (an-*drom*-a-kee) Hector's wife.

Aphrodite (aff-ro-*die*-tee) Goddess of love. Daughter of Zeus. Very beautiful. She helps to bring about the Trojan War by promising Paris that if he picks her as the fairest of the goddesses, he can marry Helen. She supports the Trojan side in the war.

Apollo (a-*poll*-o) God of the sun, healing, music and the arts. Son of Zeus, brother of Artemis. Sent a plague on the Greek army after they stole Chryseis. Supports Trojan side in the war.

Artemis (*are*-tem-iss) Goddess of hunting. Daughter of Zeus, sister of Apollo. Demands sacrifice of Iphigenia, but relents at the last minute.

Athene (a-*thee*-nee) Goddess of wisdom and war. Daughter of Zeus. Supports the Greek side in the war.

Automedon (or-*tom*-a-don) Achilles's chariot-driver.

Balius (*bal*-ee-us) *see* **Xanthus**

Briseis (briss-*eh*-iss) Achilles's servant girl, taken by Agamemnon to replace his own girl, Chryseis. This leads to an argument between the two men and Achilles's withdrawal from the fighting.

Calchas (*kal*-cass) A soothsayer (someone who can see into the future) who accompanies the Greek army to Troy.

Cassandra (kass-*an*-dra) Daughter of Priam and Hecuba, sister of Hector, Paris and Polydorus. Has psychic powers.

Chiron (*khee*-ron) A centaur (half man and half horse), renowned for his wisdom. He taught Achilles and other Greek heroes.

Chryseis (kriss-*eh*-iss) Daughter of Chryses. She is taken by Agamemnon to be his servant girl, but is returned later to appease Apollo.

Chryses (*kry*-seez) Priest at one of Apollo's temples. Father of Chryseis.

Clytemnestra (kly-tum-*nes*-tra) Wife of Agamemnon and mother of Iphigenia.

Diomedes (die-o-*mee*-dees) One of the Greek leaders.

Eris (*air*-iss) Goddess of spite. Causes the Trojan War by bringing the golden apple to the wedding of Peleus and Thetis, because she hasn't been invited.

Hector (*hek*-tor) Son of Priam and Hecuba. Leader of the Trojan army. Kills Achilles's friend, Patroclus, and is killed by Achilles.

Hecuba (*hek*-yoo-ba) Queen of Troy, wife of Priam and mother of Hector, Paris, Polydorus and Cassandra.

Helen (*hell*-en) Wife of Menelaus and lover of Paris. Considered to be the most beautiful woman in the world. Had a lot of admirers before her marriage, including Ulysses. Menelaus starts the war against Troy because Helen runs away with the Paris to Troy. At the very end of the Trojan War Menelaus takes her back.

Hephaestus (heff-*eest*-us) Blacksmith of the gods. Makes splendid shield, sword and helmet for Achilles.

Hera (*hee*-ra) Queen of the gods and wife of Zeus. Very jealous of Zeus's dealings with other women and goddesses. Supports the Greek side in the war.

Hermes (*her*-mees) Messenger of the gods and son of Zeus.

Hesione (hess-*eye*-on-ee) Sister of Priam, captured by the Greeks.

Idaius (id-*ay*-us) Priam's wagon driver on his journey to the Greek camp to ask Achilles for Hector's body.

Iphigenia (if-ij-a-*nee*-a) Daughter of Agamemnon and Clytemnestra. Almost sacrificed to Artemis by her father in order to make the wind blow so that the Greek ships can set sail, but saved at the last minute and sent to one of Artemis's temples to be a priestess.

Lycomedes (lie-*com*-a-deez) King of Skyros, the island where Thetis hides Achilles from the Greeks.

Menelaus (me-ne-*lay*-us) King of Sparta, brother of Agamemnon, husband of Helen and one of the Greek leaders. He declares war on Troy when Helen runs away with Paris.

Nereus (*nee*-ryoos) Sea god, father of Thetis.

Nymphs (*nimphs*) Demigoddesses, (only one parent is a god or goddess) spirits of water, trees and mountains.

Palamedes (pa-la-*mee*-dees) Greek soldier. Goes to Ithaca to track down Ulysses and tricks him into agreeing to join the army.

Pandarus (*pan*-da-rus) Trojan soldier. Spurred on by Athene, he fires an arrow at Menelaus, thus breaking a truce and causing the war to continue.

Paris (*pa*-riss) Son of Priam and Hecuba. Brother of Hector, Polydorus and Cassandra. The gods predicted at his birth that he would bring destruction to Troy, so his parents abandoned him on Mount Ida, where he was rescued by shepherds. Ordered by Zeus to choose the fairest of the three goddesses Hera, Athene and Aphrodite, he picks Aphrodite. In return she promises him the most beautiful woman in the world as his wife. He returns to Troy and is welcomed by his parents. On a visit to Greece he falls in love and runs away with Menelaus's wife, Helen (the most beautiful woman in the world). This leads to the Trojan War, which eventually causes the destruction of Troy.

Patroclus (pa-*troc*-lus) Greek soldier, comrade and best friend of Achilles. Goes into battle instead of Achilles, and is killed by Hector.

Peleus (*pee*-lyoos) King of Phthia, husband of Thetis, and father of Achilles.

Penelope (pen-*ell*-o-pee) Queen of Ithaca and wife of Ulysses.

Polydorus (poll-ee-*door*-us) Youngest son of Priam and Hecuba. Killed by Achilles.

Priam (*pry*-am) King of Troy, husband of Hecuba, and father of Hector, Paris, Polydorus and Cassandra.

Sinon (*sy*-non) Greek soldier. Pretends to be a deserter when the Greek army sails away from Troy, and tricks the Trojans into bringing the wooden horse into Troy.

Sleep God of sleep.

Thetis (*thet*-iss) A goddess and sea nymph. Wife of Peleus and mother of Achilles. Tries to make her son immortal when he is a baby by dipping him into the River Styx, but forgets to immerse the heel that she's holding him by.

Ulysses (*yoo*-liss-ees) Also known as Odysseus (o-*dee*-si-us) King of Ithaca, husband of Penelope. He tries to avoid joining the Greek army by pretending to be insane, but this fails. Becomes a great leader, renowned for his cleverness and cunning. He comes up with the idea for the wooden horse which leads to the destruction of Troy and the Greek victory.

Xanthus and Balius (*zan*-thus and *bal*-ee-us) Achilles's golden horses.

Zeus (*zyoos*) King of the gods. Married to Hera who is also his sister. Rules from Mount Olympus, often influences human lives. All-powerful.

IMPORTANT PLACES

Aulis City where the Greek armies gather before setting off for Troy.

Mount Ida Mountain near Troy where Paris grew up as a shepherd boy.

Ithaca Island kingdom, home of King Ulysses and Queen Penelope.

Mycenae Kingdom of King Agamemnon.

Mount Olympus The high mountain where the Ancient Greeks believed Zeus and most of the gods and goddesses lived.

River Scamander River flowing through Troy and to the sea.

Skyros Island where Thetis hides Achilles from the Greeks.

Sparta Kingdom of King Menelaus.

River Styx Magical river in the Land of the Dead, which can make those who bathe in it immortal.

Troy Huge fortified city, home of King Priam and Queen Hecuba, where Helen was taken after she ran away with Paris. Site of the Trojan War.

For information regarding permission, write to Usborne Publishing Ltd., Usborne House, 83-85 Saffron Hill, London, EC1N 8RT, England.
First published in Great Britain in 1998 by Usborne Publishing Ltd.

ISBN   0-439-32644-3

Copyright © 1998 by Usborne Publishing Ltd. All rights reserved.
Published by Scholastic Inc., 555 Broadway, New York, NY 10012, by arrangement with Usborne Publishing Ltd.
The name Usborne and the device are Trade Marks of Usborne Publishing Ltd.
SCHOLASTIC and associated logos are trademarks and/or registered trademarks of Scholastic Inc.

12 11 10 9 8 7 6 5 4 3 2   2 3 4 5 6/0

Printed in the U.S.A.   09

First Scholastic printing, October 2001